UNHINGED

The Amygdala Syndrome 2

JACK HUNT

DIRECT RESPONSE PUBLISHING

Published by Direct Response Publishing

ISBN: 9781794551404

Also By Jack Hunt

The Renegades
The Renegades 2: Aftermath
The Renegades 3: Fortress
The Renegades 4: Colony
The Renegades 5: United
Mavericks: Hunters Moon
Killing Time
State of Panic
State of Shock
State of Decay
Defiant
Phobia
Anxiety
Strain
Blackout
Darkest Hour
Final Impact
And Many More…

Dedication

For my family.

Chapter 1

A bead of blood trickled down her neck as Jenna Jackson held the shard of mirror to her throat. She'd purposely cut the skin. Not too deep but enough to get their attention. Anything to make it clear she meant business. She wasn't messing around. Not anymore. The thought of ending her life had crossed her mind countless times since arriving at the CDC in Chicago. She'd wasn't suicidal but the thought of going through one more test, and enduring excruciating pain, was unbearable.

It had been four, maybe five days since they'd arrived. It was hard to keep track of the time because there were no clocks on the wall, and the doctors refused to tell her.

They were merciless in their pursuit of the cure, and

she didn't think for one moment that they wouldn't kill her if it meant discovering the answer. Pete Douglas was a prime example of that. He'd died three days after arrival. They never told her how it happened, he simply never returned. It was because of this that she was convinced she was next. She wouldn't have minded if it had been as simple as taking a blood sample but it wasn't. They had prodded, poked, extracted and performed all manner of tests, many of which had left her with bruising, cuts and agonizing headaches. Jenna had vomited, shit herself and hallucinated due to the crap they'd pumped through her veins.

But no more.

She wouldn't take it.

It all ended that morning. Morning? Was it morning? In all truth she didn't know. She hadn't seen daylight since the day before being taken from Alpine. They'd locked her away like a caged criminal.

Hell, even criminals in prisons had more rights than her.

Her living quarters were atrocious. They had kept her in a thirteen by ten room with nothing more than a hard bed and a large two-way mirror that separated her from another room. It made her feel like a fish in a bowl. There wasn't even a bathroom. She had to get permission to piss and even when she did, they wanted a sample. No, this was her hell. Cold floors, whitewashed concrete walls, and hardened steel. Outside her room two soldiers were always on guard, protecting the United States' most valuable commodity. That's what she was now. No longer a human, just a commodity that would be bought and sold. She knew that if they ever found the cure, they weren't going to give it out freely. Someone at the top would find a way to use it as a bargaining chip. They would take advantage of the moment. Of course, someone would argue that wouldn't be the case. No, people were good at heart. But that was ideal thinking and they no longer lived in an ideal world. In a matter of days, the country had been overtaken, state by state.

When she wasn't being poked by doctors, they had her

hooked up to a monitor. Everywhere she went she was under the watchful eye of cameras. Two in her room, two in the bathroom and many throughout the facility. She still hadn't figured out exactly where she was. Sure, she'd been told it was the CDC but it looked more like a hospital. Without windows it was hard to tell if she was above or below ground. In the times they would escort her from her cell to surgical hell, she'd heard various sounds, mostly dull knocking and elevators in operation. The whole place was powered by generators because according to Colonel Lynch the grid was down in various parts of the country — the outbreak had spread beyond Texas and had already decimated what little infrastructure had remained.

That's why she was important.

Everything they were doing was for her protection.

She was now their only hope.

Salvation. That's what Colonel Lynch had said. She was going to save the world. Well she didn't feel like a savior. More like a martyr, taking all the punishment to find the cure. Well it ended today. She had cooperated enough and what was she getting out of it? Shitty food, zero company, dismal living conditions and lies, nothing but lies. She hadn't even seen the two men who had traveled with her to Chicago. They were separated the moment the Chinook landed. Her only companion had been Pete and he was now dead. At least that's what she believed.

"You are important. Special, even," Lynch had said. *"No one else has managed to survive the disease."*

And by disease she meant the genetically manufactured screwup that the military had put together. A weak ass attempt at creating a drug that would make soldiers fearless and reduce anxiety. Something that was compiled in a lab from a disease known as Urbach-Wiethe. On the surface it sounded all well and good but like anything that the government got its hands on, they found a way to make mistakes. And what a mistake they had made. The contagious pandemic had spread and it was beginning to gain momentum with each passing day. Anyone who became infected was unstable. Their natural survival instinct of fight-or-flight was out of whack. Like a pendulum swinging back and forth it caused people to swing from fearless curiosity through to fearful aggression. Both were dangerous. Both were bringing the nation to its knees. It wouldn't be long before the rest of the world would know its effect.

Instability brought its own set of problems.

There was no way to know who to trust. Who would flip out? Would they harm themselves or someone else? It was hard to know. Then there was the little fact that anyone who became infected died within 72 hours. Though, according to Lynch, that may have changed. Several of the infected who they were testing over the past few days were still alive after that period of time, leading them to believe the disease had morphed. Now waiting for the infected to die was no longer an option. Jenna had managed to get one of the nurses to talk to her and tell her what was going on outside the building. She'd said she didn't want to know. It was safer inside. The streets of

Chicago had been turned into a war zone. The military were out eradicating as many of the infected as possible. But it wasn't just them they had to worry about. Regular people struggling to survive in the new world were taking matters into their own hands. And gangs, nefarious groups and the bottom dwellers of society were taking advantage of a nation at its weakest.

The only upside to it was that it wasn't airborne. Had it been, it would have spread faster. No, the infection spread via blood or saliva, at least that's what they'd been able to determine so far. And with so much blood being spilled in the streets, becoming one of the infected had just become even easier. Once infected, people would go through a variety of changes. It would affect their memory, their body and their sense of fear. Moving them from being frozen by fear to lashing out. The body would produce symptoms within the first six hours that resembled the flu — headaches, cough, runny nose, watery eyes and fever. After twelve, the skin and eyes would change and they would become violent.

Except that never happened to Jenna. She didn't experience the symptoms. She'd been exposed to the infected, even had blood and saliva end up in her mouth from a fight with one, but it had done nothing. Her body had fought off the infection, resisted and remained normal. She wasn't the only one. There were others, five more, but they had all died in one way or another.

Anyway, that's why she was here.

Chicago. At the CDC, wherever the CDC was in the city. She wished she could go out, breathe in fresh air and see sunlight. She'd asked but they refused. They said it was too dangerous. Yeah, for them, she thought.

They weren't the one stuck inside getting needles jabbed in them, they weren't the one having blood and samples extracted from all over her body. She didn't think a person could experience the amount of pain they'd put her through but now she knew.

Day after day, hour after hour, she'd been strapped down and run through a battery of tests and in all instances, she hadn't been sedated. They didn't want anything to interfere with their results.

When she wasn't staring up at a ceiling screaming in agony, they would send her back to her room and isolate her. It was another test. They wanted to reduce the stimulus of the eyes. As for her other senses? They had taken that to the extreme by placing her in a float tank filled with several inches of saltwater. She'd laid there for close to four hours until her skin was wrinkled and felt on fire. She had no idea what they hoped to achieve but it had led to her hallucinating. She'd seen Brody, Nick and even had a conversation with her dead son Will.

Where were they now? The last she remembered, Brody, Gottman and Michael had headed for Marfa to find Nick. Had they found him? Had they died trying to get to him? Were they now infected? There hadn't been a day that had passed that she hadn't thought about her son. She'd heard the conversation in the Chinook on the way to Chicago about wiping out the two towns. The thought of losing her family at the hands of the military only made her more and more angry.

Jenna tried to get answers.

When would this end?

Why hadn't they made a cure?

When could she see her family again?

Why did they still need her if they'd already taken samples?

But they refused to speak to her. Jenna was convinced Lynch was behind it. She hadn't seen that bitch except for a few times over the past week, and that was only when she wanted to get an update on their progress. Jenna had tried the polite route but that had got her nowhere. It was time for a new strategy.

"Back off or I do it!" Jenna said. Five minutes earlier Jenna had been brought down for another session in the torture chamber, at least that's what she called it. They'd strapped in her left arm and were in the process of doing her right arm when she lashed out. They never expected it as she'd always been so compliant. It wasn't that she didn't want to fight back but she knew if she didn't kick up a fuss the soldiers would eventually back off and become lax in their duties. That was what she had been waiting for. All she was doing was biding her time, holding out for the right moment, and that day had finally arrived.

After cracking the doctor in the face, and rearing back her leg and driving it into a nurse's stomach, she'd managed to get out of her one restraint and smash a mirrored window nearby. Even as two soldiers rushed into the room with rifles raised and bellowing out commands, she didn't relent. Jenna knew they wouldn't kill her.

She was the last hope.

The golden egg.

Salvation for humanity.

They'd already messed up killing the other immune, were they really going to make that same mistake? No. Not this time. She watched as the doctors and nurses exited fearing for their lives.

"Put it down!" the soldier commanded.

Jenna backed up. "I want to speak to Lynch."

“You can. Just drop what’s in your hand.”

“Don’t lie to me. I’m tired of your lies.”

“I’m not lying. We’ll contact her but I need you to—”

“Not until I see that bitch,” Jenna said cutting them off. “I want answers.”

After multiple failed attempts at negotiating with her, one of the soldiers backed out of the room leaving the other eyeballing her and adjusting his grip on his M4. Beads of sweat rolled down his face. Jenna could tell it wasn’t her he feared but his superior. She was just a 140-pound woman with a shard of mirror. It didn’t take long for Lynch to appear. When she came into the room she immediately acted as if she was going to talk her down from the ledge. That same attitude of superiority permeated the atmosphere. “All right, Jenna. That’s enough theatrics for one day. Put the mirror down and let’s talk like adults.”

“Fuck you. I want answers. What happened to Pete?”

“Pete was moved to a different facility.”

“Liar. Tell me the truth. He’s dead, isn’t he?”

Lynch glanced back at the two-way mirror. Who was behind it? Who was watching?

"Jenna." Lynch moved forward a few steps with her hands out. "We can discuss that once you have put that down."

"I have been prodded, poked, injected with different liquids and made to digest all manner of shit. And for what? To be sent back to an empty room. Refused simple rights. No. We do this my way now. I want to know what happened to Pete. I want to know what happened to the two men I arrived with. I want to see daylight. I want to be let out of that cell for more than your tests. I want a room with my own bathroom. I want to know when this torture will stop. I want better food. I want—"

"Okay. Okay!" Lynch yelled throwing up her hands. Jenna could tell she wasn't breaking her down. A look of anger flashed on Lynch's face making it clear that she was just pretending to give a shit. As soon as Jenna put that shard on the ground it would be back to the old ways.

Well she wasn't going back. She'd rather be dead.

"If you haven't found a cure by now, continuing your tests isn't going to help."

"Jenna. There are few people like you in the world."

"Yeah, yeah, I'm special. Save that speech for someone who gives a shit. If this is how you treat special people then I don't want to know how you're treating the two men I came here with."

"They are fine. Perfectly fine. They are guests."

"Where are they? I want to see them."

Lynch sighed and turned and whispered into the ear of the one soldier closest to her. He disappeared. When she turned back she said, "You have to understand that what we are doing here is for the good of humanity. If anyone should realize the gravity of this situation it's you. You're a nurse for God's sake!"

"I don't need you preaching at me. Searching for answers is one thing, stripping a person of human dignity is another. This is a human rights violation. But let me guess, Amnesty doesn't know about me, right?" She smiled and adjusted her grip on the shard. It was beginning to cut into her hand. More blood trickled down her wrist causing Lynch to look even more disturbed.

"I'm just saying we are doing the best we can under these conditions. You haven't seen what is happening out there right now. Believe me, you might think you have it bad in here but you would be wrong."

Right then the soldier returned, this time with the two men from the truck that had picked them up — Sergio and Lars. Their eyes widened as they saw her, then darted to Lynch. "See. Here they are. You're good, right, guys?" she asked without taking her eyes off Jenna.

"As good as can be," Sergio replied. "What's going on here?"

"Just a little misunderstanding. Isn't that right, Jenna?" Lynch said.

"Have you seen outside?" Jenna asked Sergio.

He nodded. "From the roof. It's bad."

A smile formed on Lynch's smug face. Jenna wanted to wipe it off and replace it with agonizing pain. Anything to make her feel what she had endured over the past five days.

"I want to be put with them. Have the same rights. I will continue to comply with the tests but I want a few things: books, better sleeping conditions, better food, answers to what has happened to my family, and more time outside, and the company of these men." She didn't know them but they were from the same town as her and if that was the only tie she had, the only sense of comfort she could find, she would take it.

"That's a lot to ask for."

Jenna cut deeper into her skin causing more blood to run down.

Lynch's nostrils flared and she put a hand out. "Okay. Okay. You've got it." She motioned to one of the soldiers. "Put her with the others." Then she looked back at Jenna. "Now would you put that down?"

"Not until I'm out of your sight. Now get the hell out!" Jenna said, jabbing her finger towards the exit and finding satisfaction in telling Lynch where to go. She watched with a look of glee on her face as Lynch backed out of the room, a frown forming on her brow.

Sergio and Lars strolled over and guided her out of the room.

She was free. At least for now.

The first part of her strategy had worked. Now it was time for the final piece — escape.

Chapter 2

The sedan screamed forward until it smashed into the wall, turning the 200-pound crazed man into pâté. "Nick. Nick!" a voice yelled as the world came back into view. The sound of the engine ticking over, a hiss, and the smell of burning attacked his senses. He could feel something wet dripping down the side of his face as the driver's door swung open and someone helped him upright. Ahead, the crazed lunatic lay slumped over the hood, and the windshield was partially smashed from where he'd attempted to hack his way in with an axe. Jasper appeared at his side followed by Devan.

"You okay, man?" Devan asked reaching in and ruffling his hair.

He shook his head, and brought a hand up to his forehead. He glanced at the blood and felt his stomach churn. His skull was throbbing and his vision slightly blurred.

"I thought you were dead," Jasper added.

Nick slid out, and then felt pain shoot through him. "Remind me never to do that again," he said gripping the back of his neck.

"It's whiplash. My old man got into a crash a few years back. He spent a crap load of cash getting adjustments at a chiropractor, followed by acupuncture," Jasper said.

"Acupuncture doesn't work," Devan said.

"Why, you tried it?"

"Don't need to. Anyone knows sticking needles in you does nothing."

"Actually, there is a science that proves it works."

"Yeah, I bet you said that about that ten-dollar haircut of yours."

Nick ignored them as he walked around and took a closer look at the guy.

"Guessing we should say something," Jasper said coming up behind him. "You know, a little something to send him on his way."

"Yeah, like sucks to be you," Devan said before

cracking up laughing and slapping Jasper on the back.

Nick had killed his fair share of people in the five days since they had left Alpine but that didn't mean he didn't give a shit. He couldn't help but wonder who they were, what they were like before their body was infected, their mind distorted. "This was someone's father, brother maybe, son for sure," Nick added.

"Yeah, well that asshole came this close to killing me," Devan said holding up a finger and thumb and over exaggerating. He followed up by spitting on the dead man. "So good riddance!" Devan turned and walked away leaving Jasper and Nick alone. They'd been out scavenging for supplies in the small town of Loraine, Texas. They'd been staying in a dilapidated motel just on the outskirts of Loraine while his father and Ray Gottman healed up from gunshot wounds. His father was doing better than Gottman and they could have pressed on and his father wanted to, but Emerick wouldn't have any of it. *No, we need you healed up. If Chicago is anything like the last few towns we have gone through we'll need all the help we can get.* So that left just a few of them to scavenge for supplies. Emerick was scouting for food on the east side of town while they were tackling the matter of gasoline on the west. That was where pâté man came into it. They were siphoning gas from what appeared to be an abandoned truck, when the lunatic came out of nowhere swinging an axe like Paul Bunyan. Jasper narrowly missed getting his head lopped off, and had it not been for the quick actions of Nick, Devan would have been lying in a pool of blood. Both hadn't been paying attention to their surroundings. Devan was yapping like usual, and Jasper was as blind as a bat without his glasses. That morning he'd taken a nasty fall and they'd broken. Needless to say, both came close to death. Now Nick was packing a firearm but ammo was running low and Emerick was adamant that they were only to use bullets in worst-case situations. According to Jasper this wasn't one. Their instructions were clear — run first; if you can't run, fight; if you can't fight, shoot. Not exactly rocket science but easier said than done when someone is chasing you down with an axe. Fortunately, the keys were in the ignition, and the rest was history.

"Is he always like that?" Jasper asked.

"Like what?"

"A dick."

"Ah, you get used to it," Nick said before stepping closer to get a better look at the man. Jasper placed a cautious hand on his shoulder.

"Remember what Emerick said."

"I don't think he was infected."

"He attacked us. Of course he was."

Nick shook his head. "But look at him. His skin is fine, his eyes are normal."

"It looks that way before they change, remember?"

"What if he wasn't?"

"Wasn't?" Jasper asked.

"Infected." Nick turned and looked at the vehicle and then made his way back to the driver's side. He peered in and looked in the back. It was empty. He wasn't hallucinating, was he? When he'd entered the vehicle in the heat of the moment, when the guy was trying to sever limbs, he'd heard a child whimpering. The roar of the engine as it started had blocked out the sound but…he trailed off as Jasper interrupted his train of thinking.

"Nick, what's the matter?"

Without replying to Jasper, he pulled the lever for the trunk and went around. He lifted and then staggered back a little. There in the rear was a child, no older than ten years of age. She cowered back at the sight of Nick and Jasper looking in.

"What the hell?"

"Hey bozos, you coming or not?" Devan yelled from a block away.

"What do we do now?"

Nick didn't respond. He stared at the girl, his thoughts swirling.

"Nick."

"I don't know. Okay?" he raised his voice. Jasper was constantly looking for direction as if he was leading them. He wasn't. Neither was Devan. None of them were in charge.

"It's okay. No one is going to hurt you."

Nick stepped forward and put out his hand. Before he could get any closer he felt a hand grab him from behind and yank him back. The force was so strong it knocked him off balance and he found himself looking up at Devan.

"Are you out of your mind?" Devan asked before glancing into the back of the sedan.

"It's a girl."

"I can see that, dumbass. But she could be infected. Just like..."

"Just like her father?" Nick spat out.

They stared at one another before Devan continued, "Yeah. Like him."

Nick got back up and walked closer to the trunk. "And what if he wasn't infected? Huh?"

"Then. Well. Then he shouldn't have swung an axe at us."

Nick placed both hands on his head and took a few

steps back and started hyperventilating. "I…" He was beginning to unravel. It was one thing to kill those who were infected, they would die eventually anyway, but another to kill a random person trying to protect his daughter.

"Nick, get a hold of yourself," Devan said walking over and clasping him by the shoulders.

"That could be his daughter."

Devan shrugged as if it was no skin off his nose. "What if it is? How the hell are we meant to know? You know as well as I do there is a period when they are unstable. They fluctuate back and forth between fearless and fearful. We didn't exactly have time to check him for symptoms or ask him how his week had been."

"He's right, Nick," Jasper said trying to defuse the situation.

"Of course, I'm right. What we do now, we do to survive. This isn't the Texas it was five days ago. This shit is out of control. People are unhinged. Deranged. If it comes down to my life or theirs, I'm going to be the one standing. You got it?" He stared at Nick and then placed a hand on his shoulder. "He had an axe, man. You did what you thought was best for us. If it wasn't for your quick thinking, it might be us that was decapitated."

They all looked back inside the trunk at the girl.

"So, what do we do about her?" Jasper asked.

"Nothing," Devan said. "We get the hell out of here before more trouble finds us." He nudged Jasper. "Grab the gasoline can. We'll take what we have and go."

Jasper picked it up and Devan began walking away, leaving Nick staring at the girl. "Nick!" Devan bellowed.

Nick turned and slowly began to walk away. He made it twenty yards and then stopped. "No, it's not right."

He pulled up his N-95 mask that was dangling by elastic around his neck and put it on. His hands were already gloved as he approached the vehicle and reached inside. "Come on, we won't hurt you."

"You know what, buddy. You can keep your distance from here on out. It's your ass that is on the line when we get back. Don't be surprised if my old man kicks you out of the group."

"Your old man is not in charge."

"Oh no? Well it sure isn't your father. He's been sitting around on his ass this whole time."

"He was hit with a bullet, you dumbass!" Nick said as he pulled the girl out. Her face was dirty, her clothing stained and there was something funky in her hair, like grease. "What's your name?"

Her large blue eyes darted between him and Devan who was now leering over him.

"She hasn't got a name. Leave her be."

"Would you shut up!"

He heard Devan groan and then walk away cursing.

Nick dropped down to a knee. "My name's Nick Jackson. You?"

"Mia."

"Mia…?"

"Just Mia."

He raised an eyebrow. "Look, uh…" he trailed off unsure of what to say to her. Did he tell her that he'd just killed her father? Did he offer to take her back? No. "Where is your mother?"

"I don't know."

"Who put you in the trunk?"

"My father."

His stomach sank. This wouldn't end well.

"Where is he?" she asked, trying to look around.

"He's…"

Before he could lie to her, she pulled away and made it a few steps around the side of the car and then stopped. "Daddy." She repeated herself as she moved forward and then screamed, scrambling up onto the roof of the car. That only made it worse. Every scream cut through Nick like a razor blade. What had he done? He had no other choice. The guy had given him no other choice. Why didn't he say he wasn't infected? Or maybe he was. Nick didn't know what to believe anymore.

"Nick, we need to go. Devan is right. We can't afford to lose this gasoline and it's unsafe out here."

Jasper began walking away but he couldn't.

He couldn't in good faith turn his back knowing that he had killed someone and left a child without anyone. Nick went over to her and tried to get her to release her grip but she held on for dear life, sobbing into the crook of the bloodied man's neck.

"Mia. Where is the rest of your family?"

It took her several minutes before she answered. In the meantime, Devan and Jasper kept an eye on the road. Devan would flash him a scowl every so often, making it clear that he was not on board with the idea of bringing her back. The little girl shook her head.

"You don't have anyone?"

"An auntie but she's not from here."

"Where then?"

"I don't know."

He ran a hand over his head in frustration and blew out his cheeks before reaching over and taking her arm. He gave it a small tug but she wouldn't release her grip.

"Nick. We got company. Come on!"

He looked off down the road and saw a large knot of

people heading their way on foot. “Mia. Please. Come with us.”

She wouldn’t listen and there was no way in hell he was going to leave her there for the deranged or depraved. He grabbed her up, prying her fingers loose as she screamed. Her screams only got the attention of the lunatics. There was no telling if they were infected or not. But one thing was for sure, they weren’t looking to make friends. Nick flung her over his shoulder, wrapped a hand over her mouth to quench the cries, held on for dear life and began to sprint.

He was beginning to understand why his father didn’t want to stop. Stopping meant trouble and they’d already experienced enough of it. Things weren’t getting any better. Every day, every hour that passed saw the breakdown of society. They could trust no one. At some point they would need to get back on the road and soon. One thousand three hundred and seventy-four miles to Chicago was a hell of a long way to travel under normal conditions. And these were no ordinary circumstances.

What should have taken a couple of days of driving had been delayed by heavy military presence. Roving patrols, frequent checkpoints and towns east of Alpine with power had forced them off I-44, and into an endless cycle of seeking out gasoline, food, ammo and avoiding the infected. It was tough, and the odds were stacked against them but they were expecting that. It just didn't help that they now had to deal with the desperate.

Nick cast a glance over his shoulder as the crowd broke into a run. He listened for a gunshot, expecting them to shoot, but if one was fired, he didn't hear it. Was there a way out of this madness? Would society ever return to normal? *God, I hope so.*

Chapter 3

The final image of his father haunted him day and night. Ray Gottman sat outside the Route 66 Motel smoking a cigarette and reminiscing about his childhood as the sun rose over the town. He hadn't slept much that night, or the previous four nights for that matter. Memories of seeing his father at the hospital kept replaying in his mind. Although he thought he had come to terms with potentially losing him, the reality never set in. From an early age Tim Gottman had been the one man he'd looked up to. It was him who'd taught Ray to be wary of women, it was him who had inspired him to a career in law enforcement. With no siblings, no wife, and no children, his father was the only family he had, and now he was gone.

"How's the leg?"

Gottman cast a sideways glance as Brody Jackson emerged from one of the rooms. He rolled around his injured shoulder and looked out across the empty lot. They'd stashed the Humvee inside a wooded area, a few miles down the road, to avoid drawing attention.

"Better than it was five days ago. It's still painful. You?"

Brody slumped down beside him. "Surprisingly good. You seen Nick?"

"He left early this morning with Emerick. They've gone to find food and supplies."

Brody nodded. Gottman offered him a cigarette but he declined.

"I quit."

"Really, when?"

"Not long after the academy. Jenna had always been harping on at me to quit."

Gottman stared at his cigarette and rolled it around in his hand. "Women. They always want to change us."

"You sound jaded," Brody said leaning back and breathing in the humid morning air. "I didn't think the Don Juan of the dating world gave a crap about what women thought."

He grinned and took another hit on his cigarette before blowing gray smoke out the corner of his mouth. "I don't."

"You're up early today."

"Couldn't sleep. I um…keep seeing my old man."

Brody looked at him and nodded. "You okay?"

Gottman raised his eyebrows. "Yeah. Just…" he trailed off deciding not to go into it. Instead, he shifted the topic to something else. "What if she's not there, Brody?"

"She will be."

"I admire your confidence, chief, but you and I both know that only gets you so far."

"She has to be," Brody replied changing his response. "And stop calling me chief."

"Fine. It's been five days and we are still another eleven hundred miles from Chicago. Even if we leave today, we could be looking at least another two to three days and that's if we're lucky. It was bad five days ago, but I'm guessing it's a hell of a lot worse now."

"Well that's why I recommended not stopping."

"Hey, you know I would have kept going but Emerick..."

"Yeah, Emerick."

Right then Callie emerged from a motel room. She was wearing flats, jeans, and a loose white sweater.

Brody gave a nod. "Hey there, sweetheart. Did you sleep well?"

She pawed at her eyes. "Yeah. Where is everyone?"

"They went into town to do a supply run."

She groaned. "I said I wanted to go the next time."

"I know you did but..."

"But they didn't think I couldn't handle it."

"I wasn't going to say that," Brody replied before Callie walked off leaving both of them speechless.

"You think it's a good idea bringing her along?" Gottman asked.

"She lost both of her parents. We couldn't leave her there."

Gottman took a drag and blew out smoke. "We left a

lot of people behind."

"Yeah, and we had good reason." Brody rose. "You need to remember we're not cops anymore, Gottman."

With that said he walked off.

"Where you going?"

"To speak with Callie, and stretch my legs."

"You want me to come with you?" Gottman reached for his crutch.

Brody waved him off. "No. I'm good."

Gottman nodded and leaned back trying to forget the past.

* * *

Not far from the motel was a small pond and a kids park that had fallen into disrepair. Callie was leaning on the edge of a wooden bridge that went over the pond. She looked at him and straightened up as he approached. "You know, I used to take Nick to a place like this back when we lived in El Paso. Strange how certain places look similar," Brody said looking around. Callie didn't reply but just gazed into the dirty water. He could see the pain in her. It wasn't easy to lose family, especially family.

"How old are you, Callie? Eighteen?"

"I turn eighteen in two months."

He nodded, leaning against the bridge and looking at the lily pads.

"I wasn't that much younger than that when I lost my mother." She glanced at him with piqued interest. "She passed away from breast cancer." He shook his head.

"How did you cope?" she asked.

"Not very well. But you get through it. It helps to have good people around you. A support system. Friends, family members who you can lean on."

Her eyebrows shot up. "Well, I'm fresh out of family."

Silence stretched between them.

"You want to talk about it?"

She shook her head.

"All right."

They stood there in the silence. The sun that had disappeared behind the clouds only moments earlier, came out again spreading its warmth over them. The smell of rotten eggs from the stagnant pond of floating green goo drifted up.

Callie sighed and said, "My mother was alive when I arrived at the house."

Brody turned his face towards her, while Callie didn't take her eyes off the pond.

"When I reached the house, I ran in expecting to find them alive but instead I found my dad…" She struggled to get the words out. "With multiple knives in his back. There was so much blood. So much." She shook her head, reliving the moment in her mind. Her hands began to shake and she gripped the wooden railing harder. It was traumatic for anyone to witness death but to find your own parent brutally murdered brought its own set of challenges. "After, I hurried upstairs calling out to my mother. I rushed into her room and found her sitting on the edge of the bed with a knife in her hand. She was covered in blood. I've never seen so much blood. She stared at me but said nothing. It was like she couldn't even remember who I was. I tried to get her to put the knife down but she wouldn't listen." Callie took a deep breath and Brody placed a hand on her back.

"It's okay, Callie."

"I backed up and...bumped into a piece of furniture. The next moment she was on me trying to stab me. I screamed for her to wake up. To snap out of it but she wouldn't. A vase that had fallen off the furniture was nearby. I reached for it and smashed it against her skull. If that hadn't been there I don't think I would be here. It made her drop the knife. I tried to get away but she grabbed my leg and I had no other choice but to..." Again, she trailed off though this time she put her hands out in front of her and stared at them as they shook. "I killed her. I killed my own mother."

She glanced at him and he gripped her shoulder pulling her into his chest to comfort her. Callie wrapped her arms around him and began to sob hard.

"You did what you had to."

He tried to comfort her with his words but he knew it would take more than that. That kind of trauma didn't leave a person in a matter of days, weeks or even months. She would live with it for the rest of her life, haunted by the memory. As he held her tight something caught his attention in the distance. It was the sound of an engine, then movement through the trees.

"Come. Quick. We need to move."

"What?" she asked turning.

Brody grabbed her hand and hurried back towards the motel. When he had Gottman within earshot he called out, "Get inside. There's a vehicle coming."

Gottman struggled to his feet and hobbled back into the motel using his crutch for support. Brody pulled his Glock in preparation for the worst. Over the past five days they had seen a number of people stop at the motel and go through the rooms. Each time they had exited via the back windows and stayed in the woodland until they left. They had agreed only to engage when necessary. Avoidance was the key if they wanted to survive long-term. Brody was the last inside the motel room. He closed the door behind him and told Callie to open the back window and prepare to exit while he slipped up beside the curtain and peeked out.

A beat-up 4 x 4 black pickup truck swerved quickly into the lot and three men and a woman, aged between twenty and thirty, hopped out. All of them were packing heat and wearing N-95 masks. The first thing they did was head into the main office. He could hear them making a ruckus. They were smashing items and tossing out paperwork. An office chair came crashing out of the main window and rolled across the gravel lot. A tall, skinny fella who was heavily tattooed came out with the woman. He was wearing a muscle vest, jeans, and a thick silver chain hung from his pocket. He swung a baseball bat around in his hand. A cigarette dangled from the corner of his mouth. Brody could feel his heart beating harder as the guy looked at the long line of rooms.

He watched the woman, who had short pink hair, slide up beside him and nuzzle on his neck. They pulled their masks down and sucked face for a few seconds before she bounced on the balls of her feet heading towards the first motel room.

"Head out the back," Brody said.

"You know how hard that was the last time," Gottman said. "No, fuck that. I say we take them out."

"Gottman. You're in no state to..."

"It's my leg not my arm. If anyone isn't ready, it's you," he said hobbling over to take a look.

"I'm not risking it. We've got Callie to think about."

"I can take care of myself. Give me one of the guns," Callie said.

"You've never fired one."

Her brow furrowed. "It doesn't exactly look hard."

"Spunky gal," Gottman said, a smile forming on his face before he peered out.

"No. We exit and wait for the others."

"There's four of them, three of us," Gottman said.

"Yeah, but who knows how many more of them there are. I'm not taking any risks."

"Fine. We do it your way. Let's go, Callie," Gottman said gesturing to the back of the room. She frowned but didn't argue.

Brody stayed where he was, watching the two emerge from the first room and kick in the door on the second. Their room was two more down from that. He glanced over his shoulder and saw Callie climb out and then watched as Gottman made a half-assed attempt. "Gottman, hurry up."

"Oh, I'm sorry. Am I holding things up?" he said sarcastically as he slipped out the window. Brody hurried over and tossed out his crutch. It landed on him causing Gottman to curse. It didn't take long to duck out the window. After he closed it, they waded through overgrown grass and took cover in the tree line. Brody ducked down and tried to keep an eye on the windows. From where they were located they could hear glass being shattered, and all manner of noise as the hooligans went room to room and trashed each one.

"You'd think these idiots would have better things to do with their time."

"Time has taken on new meaning now," Brody said.

In the aftermath of the outbreak, those that were infected took to the streets, some protesting the strong arm of the military who were isolating the infected and preventing others from looting. But looting was still occurring. They couldn't stop that any more than they could the pandemic that had made it beyond the borders of Alpine and Marfa. Within the first twenty-four hours of leaving for Chicago they had seen gasoline stations with signs indicating fuel sales were limited to a few gallons for each customer. Towns just outside of Alpine had power and internet for a while. Media were reporting widescale attacks in towns and cities throughout Texas. Hospitals were overwhelmed, and police were starting to halt fuel sales and guarding the pumps as violence erupted.

It didn't take long before locals began taking swings at one another and using weapons. Within forty-eight hours they had barely made progress on the interstate due to people abandoning their vehicles and fleeing on foot. Traffic slowed to a crawl and they were forced to head off the main vein and use back roads as the Humvee was drawing unwanted attention. That's what had brought them into the town of Loraine. Emerick then had the idea to hunker down for a few days to allow them to heal, and collect supplies and enough gasoline to last the remainder of the journey. Brody had fought him on it and wanted to keep going but the decision was otherwise unanimous. Even his own son thought it was best.

"Oh shit."

"What?" Brody asked.

Callie patted down her body, looking frantic.

"I left my phone in the room," Callie said. "Oh shit."

"And?"

"It has a photo of my parents on it. It's the only one I have left."

"It's too late," Gottman said. "You'll just have to hope they don't find it."

"No. I can get back in and grab it before they…"

"No, Callie," Brody said. "It's too risky."

"It's the only picture I have."

"And..."

Before he could say another word, she shot past him, running at a crouch towards the window. "Callie!" he yelled but she didn't stop or look.

"Damn it!"

"I told you. Women are crazy," Gottman said.

"Shut up, Gottman." Brody took off after her. By the time he made it out of the long grass she was already crawling through the motel window. He wanted to call out to her again but they were too close. The chance of them being heard was far greater than before. Callie disappeared inside the room as Brody made it to the window. Out of breath he placed his hands on his knees to catch his breath. His arm was aching badly as he peered in. Callie crossed the room and scooped up a phone off the table. She turned, smiled and raised it to show him before making her way back. She hadn't made it halfway across when the door burst open.

"Huh! Well look what we have here," the skinny guy said, a grin forming on his face.

Chapter 4

Glass crunched beneath his boots as Emerick Jones stepped into the town grocery store. His hopes weren't high. One glance at the place from the outside made it clear that they would be lucky to find a single can of food. Loraine only had one grocery, and a few convenience stores. For the past few days they'd been living off provisions gained from towns before the grid went down across the state of Texas. That had only lasted so long.

"I'm just saying, we could have buried him," Chad said.

Chad was referring to the soldier who was with them when they left Alpine. He'd lasted close to twenty-four hours before he succumbed to his injuries. Chad had wanted to give him a proper burial and maybe they could have but Emerick wanted to put as much distance as possible between them and the town. Who knew how much of the area the military was going to wipe out? Just on the outskirts of Fort Stockton he'd turfed the guy's body out, and rolled him into a ditch.

"I admit it wasn't a military send-off but it was the best we could give him under the circumstances," Emerick said.

"If it wasn't for him we wouldn't have the Humvee."

Emerick glanced over his shoulder at him but refused to bite. Over the past five days he'd brought it up numerous times as if he was trying to lure him into an argument.

"You go down there. I'll check out back," Emerick said breaking away and strolling down aisle three. Overturned carts littered the floor along with boxes that had been torn open. Some of it looked as if people had been fighting over it, as fruit and cereal was splattered on the floors, walls and checkout counters. A foul odor permeated the air. The place stank like cabbage and lettuce that had been left out in the sun to wilt. Chad continued to talk to him as he browsed the shelves. Because they were empty, Emerick could see him through the metal.

"He deserved better, Emerick."

Emerick couldn't hold his tongue any longer. He changed direction and made his way down to the aisle Chad was in. "You know what. If you gave a shit, why did you let us leave him back there? Huh? Why didn't you stay?"

"Common sense."

"Ah good, at least we're talking the same language now, because it was common sense to not stop and waste twenty minutes digging him a grave. It's a waste of energy burying the dead. People are dropping like flies. This is a different world. The sooner you get that through your thick skull the better."

Emerick turned to walk away and he heard a click.

He stopped moving and looked over his shoulder to see Chad aiming his rifle.

"Maybe, I'll leave your body here to rot. Hey? What do you think about that?"

Emerick smiled, strolled over to him, grabbed the end of the barrel and placed it against his own forehead. "You want to shoot me? Go ahead. Pull the trigger."

Chad stared back.

"C'mon. You think that will change things? Then do it. Do it!"

A few seconds of tension between them, before Chad lowered his weapon.

"Yeah, just as I thought. You haven't got the nerve to make the hard decisions. That's why we found you alone in that school, cowering away."

"Don't push it, Emerick."

Chad slid by him giving him a shove that forced him back into the shelf. They'd been at odds with one another ever since Alpine. Sure, he'd come back and helped them out of a tight spot but that didn't mean he trusted him. He was still military, employed by Uncle Sam and capable of turning on their group.

"Why are you staying with us? Wouldn't you be better off with your own kind?"

"My own kind?" Chad asked as he turned on his flashlight and made his way into the back of the store.

"Yeah. We've seen numerous checkpoints with military. Why are you still with us?"

Chad didn't reply but kept sweeping the darkened corners of the store with his flashlight. "I don't know. Why are you here?"

"I've known Chief Jackson a long time. If this nation is going to hell, I'd rather be alongside those I trust than those I don't."

"So don't trust the military. I get it. But I think you have me painted wrong. I might wear the uniform but that doesn't mean I agree with every decision they make."

"No, then maybe you should dump the uniform."

"Ah, so it's my gear that bothers you?" he said, picking up a can only to find it was empty. Chad tossed it and continued on peering into boxes that littered the floor. Someone had torn through the place and taken every damn thing.

"It's what it stands for."

"Yeah? And what's that? As I'm pretty sure the people who wear this are the ones that stick their neck out on the line to give you the freedom you continue to complain about."

"Stick their neck out on the line? Ah that's a good one. Stop making yourself out to be some kind of martyr. You have a choice. Half the guys who sign up are on a power trip. They've watched *Platoon* one too many times, or think they're Rambo. All ego. Most are overcompensating for small dicks. At the end of the day they're fighting wars that are funded by blood money," Emerick said.

"Please. Save that crap for your radio."

Right then Chad kicked a bunch of boxes and one of them barely moved. He tossed some empty ones out of the way and fished through to find it. That's when he caught the putrid whiff. "Ugh, dear God…" The bottom was soaked red and he assumed it was full of old meat. When he flipped open the top he jumped back. "Holy crap."

"What is it?"

Emerick moved forward and looked inside. "Sick bastards."

Inside were the severed limbs of a male. He looked to be in his late twenties. Chad backed away, a look of disgust on his face. He quickly made his way over to the loading docks and took a moment to catch his breath. Emerick sauntered over and patted him on the back. "Ah I get it now. You've got a weak stomach. Hell. Why did you sign up for the military if you can't stand the sight of blood?"

"Fuck off, Emerick."

Emerick laughed and pulled out a pack of smokes and tapped one out. He offered it to Chad and he took it. He lit Chad's before lighting his own and they looked out into the lot full of eighteen-wheeler shipping containers. All of them had been opened. Locals searching for food had emptied them out. Boxes, crates and wooden pallets were scattered across the asphalt.

"My father was in the military," Emerick said before taking a hit on his cigarette. Chad looked at him but said nothing. "He was a bit of an asshole. Spent most of his time away from home and the few times he did return he drank like a fish and was in the habit of showing us what his belt looked like. Yeah, he wasn't exactly what you'd call a family man." He sighed and tapped some ash and watched it blow away in the wind.

"You never wanted to follow in his footsteps?"

"Nope."

Chad nodded and blew out smoke. "So why the radio?"

"What other way can you reach the masses?"

"Ah, so you consider yourself a herald of truth."

"Not exactly but I believe that the people today should have a voice. It's often lost in the shuffle of life."

Chad hopped down and let his cigarette hang from his mouth as he went to the far end of one of the containers and looked inside.

"They're empty," Emerick said shaking his head.

"Maybe, but it doesn't hurt to look, right? That's what we're here for."

Chad swung his rifle around his back and hopped up into the back of one, disappearing out of view. Emerick could hear him clattering around inside as boxes were tossed out. Emerick's mind drifted to the past, back to when he was a kid. Every time his father would return from a tour, he would stare out the window waiting for him. The first few hours were usually good. He came in, greeted their mother, had dinner and would tell them stories of his time overseas. Emerick would hang on his every word. What he hadn't told Chad was that his room was full of military gear until he was twelve years of age. That was the age when military police showed up and carted his father away after almost killing his mother. It was like he witnessed two sides to him. The human and the monster. The sober and the drunkard. It was always the same. "I'm going out for a few drinks with the guys. I'll be home later." By the time he returned, he'd hear his mother and father arguing.

That soon led to violence, and eventually his incarceration.

From that day forward his mother removed from the home everything that was connected to the military. He followed suit. Taking down his posters, tossing out his father's old beret and even a few old medals he'd given him.

"You're wasting your time, Chad." Emerick tapped his cigarette and looked at the glowing end while boxes continued to be tossed out. It got more and more noisy. It sounded like Chad was throwing pallets against the side of the container.

"Hey Chad want to keep it down? You're going to attract attention."

When he got no response and the noise continued, Emerick hopped off the edge, stuck his cigarette in his mouth and strolled down to the open end. As he rounded it, he was just about to chew Chad out when he saw what was causing the problem. A large bearded guy had Chad up against the side by his neck and was smashing him repeatedly into the metal. Chad was doing his best to fight back but it was useless. The guy towered over him, and his arms looked like Chad's legs. He was dressed in a plaid shirt, a trucker's hat and dark jeans that were bunched up around black boots.

The cigarette dropped from Emerick's lips, and he reached for his firearm.

Before he had a chance to aim it, he felt a barrel press against the back of his head and heard a male voice. "I wouldn't do that if I was you. Drop it."

"Fuck," Emerick said before releasing his weapon. It clattered against the steel and a hand reached around and took it.

"Okay now get on your knees and put your hands behind your head. Slowly!"

"Look, we don't have anything."

"Are you hard of hearing?" the voice behind said. Emerick spread his hands wide and dropped down to his knees before interlocking his fingers behind his head.

"Alright, Archy. Let him go."

The large guy was choking the hell out of Chad. His face had a turned to a beet, and he was holding him up so that his toes were barely touching the floor of the container.

"Archy!"

The guy scowled and then released Chad. He coughed and spluttered, gripping his neck. Archy picked up Chad's rifle and motioned for him to get out and join Emerick. Once he was out, the man behind Emerick came into view. He was short in stature, sporting a goatee and wearing camo gear as if he'd just returned from a hunting trip. Attached to his back was a bow, and in his hand was a 9mm.

"Check their pockets."

Archy patted them down, and tossed out a pack of smokes, some beef jerky and additional ammo.

"That's all you've got?"

"I told you we didn't have anything."

"Where you coming from?" camo guy asked.

"Out west, we're heading east," Emerick said.

"You got a vehicle?"

Emerick chuckled. "Does it look like it?"

That was the wrong thing to say. A second after, he was pistol-whipped across the face. Chad went to react but was dealt with in a similar matter. Except he got to chew on the end of his own rifle. "Who else are you with?"

Emerick spat blood on the ground and then answered, "No one. It's just us."

"A civilian and a soldier traveling together. Now what's wrong with that picture?"

Emerick wanted to give him a sarcastic reply but he chose to hold his tongue.

"Archy, you find anything up there?"

"Nothing. It's empty."

"Too bad," he said before looking at them again. "Well boys, it's been nice knowing you." He lifted his weapon and aimed at Chad.

Emerick put a hand out. "Hold on. Wait!"

"For what?"

"We've got a vehicle."

"Shut up, man," Chad said.

"No, go ahead, civilian," camo guy replied.

"It's a Humvee. It's parked a few miles from here. I

can take you to it. Just leave us alive."

"Well I can't promise that but I'll take you up on the offer. Whereabouts?"

"I'll show you."

He shook his head. "No, I'm familiar with the area. Give me a rough idea, we'll find it."

"Don't tell him," Chad said before he got smacked across the face with the guy's handgun. Chad fell to his left but was then hauled up by Archy.

"You talk too much."

"So do you!" a voice said. Camo guy looked up but before he could react, a gun went off, and he slumped to the ground with a round in his forehead. Archy reacted by trying to run but there was too much open space. Another two rounds erupted and he dropped. Emerick looked up to see Devan on top of the container, and Nick and Jasper jogging over to meet them.

"Oh shit. Am I glad to see you, kid."

Devan climbed over the edge and dropped down. "I see you lived up to your potential, soldier boy," Devan said before moving past him with a grin on his face and walking over to Archy who was still alive. Archy was crawling forward but wasn't making much progress. Without any hesitation, Devan fired a round into the back of his head, then relieved him of his weapon. All of them stared on as he came back and tossed the rifle to Chad. "You can thank me later."

Chad got up from his knees and brushed himself off.

"So, did you find anything?" Jasper asked.

"Nothing. You?" Chad replied.

"Just a ten-year-old girl." He turned and waved to the opening of the loading dock. From out of the darkness a small child came into view.

"Are you serious?" Emerick said.

"Nick killed her father."

"Thanks, Devan," Nick said.

"Not a problem."

"We should get going." Nick thumbed over his shoulder.

"What's the hurry?"

"You ran into a little trouble, so did we. Except there are a lot more of them than two guys."

Emerick frowned as he pushed his Glock back into his holster and followed Nick around the store. His eyes widened as he saw in the distance a group making their way towards the grocery store.

"Yeah, I think that's our cue."

Chapter 5

Callie tried to run but the skinny freak knocked her to the ground. His girlfriend with the pink troll hair entered and squealed with delight as the guy dragged Callie across the carpeted floor and proceeded to wrestle for control. Brody's heart was hammering in his chest. Several thoughts raced through his mind — shoot, enter the window and fight them off, or wait to see what they planned to do. He cast a glance back towards Gottman who looked confused. *Shit.* This was on him. He peered inside and watched as the skinny guy got control of her, and his girlfriend held a knife up to Callie's throat.

He squeezed her cheeks. "So, what you doing here, girly? Huh? Where's your parents?"

"I don't have any."

The skinny guy nuzzled his nose into her hair and inhaled deeply before running his tongue down the side of her face. Callie flinched and kicked him in the foot before kneeing the woman and trying to make a second attempt to escape, this time out the front door. She didn't get far. The pink troll grabbed her by the hair and yanked her back. Callie collapsed on the ground and the woman jumped on top holding the knife to her throat.

"Now that was a stupid thing to do."

Callie struggled below her trying to get free.

"Stop moving or I will slit you from ear to ear." She sneered. "Bones. What are we going to do with her?"

He rubbed his foot. "Take her with us. I'm sure we can make use of her."

The woman grinned flashing her meth-looking teeth. "Maybe. But she's a stubborn one."

"Well I'm sure you can break her down," he said sitting on the edge of the bed and examining his foot. She'd driven her heel hard into the top of it and obviously damaged it. Rising, he limped over and reached down and grabbed a clump of Callie's hair, pulling her to her feet. She let out a squeal and Brody was about to react when Gottman came up behind him and put a hand on his shoulder.

"Wait. I have a better plan," Gottman said.

"Well you better act fast as I don't think…"

Right then the guy tossed Callie on the bed and told the woman to lock the door. He began to unbuckle his belt. The woman jumped on the bed and tried to hold Callie down. "Fuck the plan," Brody said. There was no time. He brought up his Glock and took aim just as the guy dropped his pants. He was standing at the end of the bed and was trying to get a leg out of his jeans when the round drilled a hole in his temple. It all happened so quick. The man's legs buckled as his lifeless body dropped, and Brody aimed at the woman. Unfortunately, shock didn't get the better of her, she reacted fast by bringing her arm around Callie's throat and using her as a human shield.

"You shoot me, I slit her throat. I swear I will."

They stared at each other, Brody from the outside, her from behind Callie. The woman barely showed a sliver of her face. The only parts that could be seen were her track marked arms from drug use. Slowly but surely she dragged Callie off the bed. Tears rolled down Callie's face, fear gripping her hard.

"Just let her go," Brody said.

The woman ignored him and continued backing up to the door.

In those final few seconds before she was able to reach for the handle, Callie reacted by grabbing the woman's arm and pulling it away. She elbowed her in the stomach and ran forward, bouncing over the mattress. The woman lunged forward to attack Callie.

"Get down!" Brody yelled.

Callie hit the ground just as he squeezed the trigger, unloading two rounds into the troll's chest. There was a few seconds of silence as Callie realized she was safe before she scrambled towards the window and with the help of Brody climbed out. No sooner had she got out when the sound of yelling could be heard, and someone thumping on the door. They knew it was the other two from the troll's group. Brody, Gottman and Callie hurried back to the tree line.

"Stay here, I'll be right back," Brody said.

"Where are you going?" Gottman asked.

"To finish this."

"But..."

"Emerick and Nick will be back soon. I can't have them walking into this."

He went to walk away and Gottman grabbed him by the arm. "You'll need my help."

"Gottman, just stay with her."

With that said he ran at a crouch to the rear of the motel. As he got closer, he could hear people yelling and cursing. He hoped he'd have the element of surprise and could pick them off from the window but by the time he looked through they were gone. The door was wide open and the bodies were still there. Brody stayed low and made his way around. He knew they were probably combing the area looking for the culprits.

"Go that way. I'll check over here."

He was closing in on the final corner of the building

when he heard the guy. He couldn't have been more than a few feet away. Brody ducked behind a large industrial dumpster and crouched down biding his time. The sound of boots drew near, just one set. He knew if he opened fire it would alert the other and he'd have a war on his hands. Instead, he pushed the Glock back into the holster and planned to take the guy down the old-fashioned way. Quietly he removed his expandable 21-inch baton and jerked his arm to get it to expand. Seconds felt like minutes as he waited. He didn't wait for the guy to walk past fully. As soon as one boot came into view, he exploded forward slamming the baton across the guy's knees. His finger must have been on the trigger as several rounds erupted before he released an AR-15 and collapsed. Brody knew he had seconds before the other guy came to his aid. He scrambled over to the rifle, scooped it up and brought the gun up.

"Don't shoot," the guy said, groaning on the ground. He held out one arm, pleading for his life. Brody wasn't given to kill anyone without reason. It went against everything that he stood for as a cop, and as a person. Maybe that would change if this new world stayed the way it was but for a brief second, he hesitated, seeing a human before him, not someone that was about to attack a young girl.

Expecting to be greeted by the guy's buddy, Brody kicked the downed guy in the face to knock him out and then pulled him back behind the dumpster to wait.

This time, however, he didn't hear boots, instead he heard an engine roaring to life. Brody got up and raced towards the front of the motel just in time to see the 4 x 4 pulling away. The driver glanced back at him and Brody unleashed several rounds taking out the back window. The truck tore away, bouncing off the curb and onto the main road before leaving nothing more than dust and grit swirling.

Brody shook his head and returned to the guy's pal who was still out cold.

He bent down and fished through his pockets.

There was some extra ammo, two packs of cigarettes

that Gottman would be happy to have, an unopened candy bar and a wallet. He pulled it out and looked inside. There was a photo of the unconscious man, along with a wife and two kids. It looked like the kind that might be taken in a Walmart. He was dressed differently. He looked respectable, clean and presentable — a far cry from the torn jeans, camo boots, leather jacket and shirt he had on. The guy's appearance had changed too. No longer was he sporting the clean-shaven look. He'd grown a fair amount of stubble. He pulled out the guy's license.

"Shawn Tremont."

Right then he groaned and began to stir.

Brody tucked it back into the wallet and dropped it beside him. He stood up and aimed the rifle at him, waiting for him to come to. He pushed him a little with his foot.

"Wake up." Shawn's eyes fluttered. As soon as he locked eyes with Brody, he put both hands up. That didn't last though. He began rubbing his knees.

"Shawn Tremont. Seems your pal decided to leave you

behind."

Shawn noticed his wallet beside him and he grabbed it up and put it back in his pocket. "He'll be back."

"With others, right?"

Shawn nodded.

"How many?"

"Twelve."

"Got yourself a small army."

"Have to stick together to survive this."

"You're right about that." Brody surveyed the area with his eyes before looking down at him again. "Where's the woman and children in the photo?"

"Dead." His eyes didn't well up with tears but he got this distant look in his eyes as if reliving the tragic event.

"They get infected?"

Shawn nodded, looking back at Brody.

"You going to shoot me?" he asked.

"That depends. You coming back?"

"No. But others will come."

Brody chuckled. "But you won't."

"I only met their group a few days ago. I don't owe them anything."

"And yet you understand that to survive you have to stick together."

Brody wasn't buying it. People said whatever they wanted to get out of trouble when he arrested them. This was no different. In fact, this was worse. He could put a bullet in him and walk away without any repercussions. Law. Order. Justice. It had all gone out the window. For how long? That was to be seen.

He jerked his head towards the front of the motel. "Get the hell out of here."

Shawn looked as if Brody was toying with him.

"You hear me?"

Shawn scrambled to his feet and hobbled away under Brody's watchful eye. As he stood there looking at him, Callie and Gottman came up from behind. "You're letting him go?"

"He wasn't a threat."

"Not now but later he might be. Where's the other

one?"

"He drove off. Left him behind."

"Huh. Got to love friends. But still, Brody, letting him go is not a good idea."

"Neither is killing every person we come across."

"They would have killed us and probably raped Callie."

"But they didn't."

Gottman sighed and ran a hand over his face. "Maybe not now but later they might."

"And maybe I would have chosen differently if we were staying, but we're not."

Gottman frowned. "We're leaving?"

"As soon as Emerick is back."

Gottman scoffed. "Well let's hope that occurs before your buddy returns." He patted him on the back and hobbled back to the room.

Callie fell in step as Brody followed. "Um. Mr. Jackson. Look, um. I'm really sorry to have caused all this trouble."

"It's okay."

"No, I mean if I hadn't gone back for that phone..." she trailed off.

"It had your parents on it. Don't worry."

He could have blamed her. He could have cut her loose because of that decision but they were only five days into this. There was a chance things would get under control. He had to believe the government wouldn't just shrink back from this but was doing everything in its power to push back the tide, contain and create safe zones. As fast as he knew this had spread, not every state would have been infected. There were still good people out there. Shawn might have been one. How many good people had fallen in with bad crowds out of a need to survive? He had to believe that.

Back in the room, Gottman pulled together what they had. Over the course of five days they hadn't managed to store much. It was mostly food, gasoline and some survival supplies like blankets, tarps, sleeping bags, a battery-powered radio, a first-aid kit, a can opener, matches, a compass and a few maps. Like many others they didn't think the nation was going to crumble around them. From what they'd learned on the radio, only six states had been infected. Canada was trying to offer assistance, as was the UK, but like anyone with a lick of sense they were treading carefully. No one wanted to put their own people at risk. FEMA had begun to set up camps along the interstates and word was beginning to spread that the military were out in full force rounding up anyone showing signs of infection. Rounding up was a polite way of saying they were killing them. Of course they wouldn't mention that. No one would ever know about what they did in Alpine or Marfa. That would all be swept under the rug and if they ever did manage to wrangle this in, Brody was certain they would have some politically palatable excuse.

"Can you imagine if they came across this while we were out? We've got to start thinking strategically about where we stay. We might have been able to survive here for five days but they weren't the first and they won't be the last. Places like this are going to become a hotspot for travelers. I think we stick to the woodland, stay off the main interstate and dump the Humvee."

"Dump the Humvee? And add weeks on to our arrival time?"

"We've wasted time being here," Gottman said.

"Have you forgotten Jenna?" Brody asked while helping him stuff a duffel bag with items.

"No. Brody. I have not forgotten Jenna. Hell, I don't think any of us have. But this is far greater than your need to find Jenna. I think we need to put this whole idea of the trip to Chicago up for vote."

"For vote?" Brody frowned. "Look, I'm not dragging anyone along. If you want to leave. Be my guest. The door is there. But I'm going to get my family."

"Family?" Gottman laughed. "That's funny."

Brody crossed his arms and stared at him waiting for him to explain.

"Well, seriously, Brody. You've been separated from Jenna for six months. Then this shit explodes and you now want to play happy family? Do you honestly think any of this is going to change her mind?"

Callie stood by the window looking out but occasionally glancing at them. She was listening in but staying out of it.

"No. I don't expect any of this will. But I know my wife, and until she says it's over, I'm—"

"It's already over, Brody. Don't you get it? A woman doesn't serve you divorce papers if she wants to stick around. She has moved on, and if you knew what was best, so would you."

"Yeah, well maybe you can jump from one relationship to another but not me." Gottman shook his head as Brody continued. "I wouldn't expect you to know. You haven't been married twenty-four years. Hell, you haven't been in a relationship longer than twenty-four days, have you?"

Gottman shook his head. "Man, you are so gullible. I don't need a ring on my finger or endure twenty-four years to know the truth."

Brody leaned against the wall staring at him as he zipped up the bag and dumped it on the floor. "The truth. Yeah? And what would that be?"

Before Gottman could reply they heard the sound of an engine.

Callie peered out. "It's Emerick."

"Well thank fuck that. I thought this conversation was going to spiral down into a therapy session," Gottman said hauling up the bag and heading out.

Chapter 6

A hard wind blew against her as she stood on top of the Chicago Medical Center. Jenna would have been lying to say that she didn't think Lynch would screw her over the very second she laid down that shard of mirror but it had worked. Lynch had her transferred out of her hospital prison into an upscale room located six levels down. It was like night and day. For the first time in five days she now had her own bathroom, a proper bed that was comfortable, a view from a locked window and company. Sergio and Lars were in rooms just down the hall from her along with several others that worked at the hospital.

The place was massive.

She was now overlooking the city. And what a sight. The medical center was located in Hyde Park on the South Side of Chicago. Fires burned out of control, smoke drifted across the city like a dark ghostly apparition, small stores on the ground had been looted and the city streets were covered in debris. For the first five minutes they said nothing to her but just let her soak in the view. Of course they weren't alone. Three armed soldiers stood by watching their every move. They'd escorted them to the roof and Lynch had made it clear that wherever they went, her men would follow. Jenna got close to the lip of the approximately ten-story building and looked at a six-car pileup far below. Dozens of vehicles had been abandoned in the street, others driven into buildings as if the drivers were attempting to escape the narrow corridors of the concrete jungle. Steel shutters that once sealed in store windows had been torn away and dragged out into the middle of the street. Garbage blew down the street like tumbleweed. Two car horns blared, and several gunshots rang out.

"It's far worse than it was two days ago," Lars said approaching her. He walked with a limp from the gunshot wound he'd received back in Alpine. He said he got it trying to fend off an attacker in one of the grocery stores but Jenna wasn't sure that was entirely the truth. Sergio remained quiet. He would look at her from time to time but mostly focused his attention on the city below. It was mesmerizing to see a city torn apart by devastation and to not hear the sound of emergency sirens.

"Does anyone go out?"

"Us? No. Soldiers do. They come and go, mostly to get more supplies. From what we've learned there is a FEMA camp not far from here."

"So, what have you guys been doing?" Jenna asked looking at them.

"They have us doing all the shitty jobs — literally. We empty garbage cans, clean bathrooms, wipe up piss and shit from toilets, and help serve food. It's not great but at least we're not out there, and they give us a warm bed and three meals a day."

Jenna frowned. "I don't get it. I understand why they kept me but you two?"

"It's called cheap labor," Sergio piped up, then took a drag on a cigarette. He had one foot on the lip of the roof and was leaning on his leg. He answered her without even looking. Even from the first day she met him, there was something about his demeanor and the way he looked at her that gave her the creeps. "Don't let Lars fool you into thinking we are grateful. I'm not. I wanted to leave here on the first day but they won't let us go," he said casting an angry look over his shoulder at the soldiers. "Those assholes follow us everywhere."

Jenna looked down. "You attempted to get out?"

"Attempted would be the key word. They keep us above the fourth floor at all times. It's not like we can jump out of a window. It's a long way," Lars said.

"What's on the lower floors?"

"The infected."

"What? But you said the soldiers go in and out."

"They do. Using the helicopter. The stairwells are blocked. Even though they have solar and fuel generators to provide power, the elevators are turned off."

Jenna shook her head looking around. Their Chinook wasn't on the roof. "Hold on a minute."

As if knowing what she was about to say, Sergio said, "We arrived by helicopter or have they addled your brain so much you can't remember?" She narrowed her eyes at him and he continued. "We didn't enter by way of the ground floor. We landed on this roof."

The night they arrived was a blur. It came to her in fragments. Being dragged out of the vehicle, strong-armed into a Chinook. The downwash of air, the loud sound of rotors. Then an injection in her arm. The rest seemed disjointed. Arriving sometime in the middle of the night. High winds. The sound of gunfire. Lots of yelling, and then fluorescent lights, being placed on a gurney and wheeled down a corridor.

She knew she was in a hospital as she saw nurses and doctors but that was it.

That was the last time she'd seen Sergio and Lars.

"Pete Douglas. Do you know what happened to him?" Jenna asked.

"Who?"

"The security guard."

"No idea. I thought he was with you."

They were confirming her worst fear that he was dead. Lynch wouldn't admit it. She said he'd been transported to a different facility but she wasn't buying that. If he was still alive she wouldn't have entered negotiations with Jenna. She turned away from the edge of the roof. She'd seen enough. The air wasn't fresh, it was putrid with the smell of smoke, death and ruin.

Back inside, she shivered.

"I can get you some fresh clothes if you like. No need to wear hospital gowns," Lars said.

"I don't know, I was beginning to like them," Sergio said craning his head back as if expecting to see her naked butt. She'd already taken care of that by putting on another one underneath the other.

Lars gave Sergio a shove and glared at him. "Show the lady some respect." They walked down a corridor and entered a stairwell. "I'll take you down to the common room. Everyone convenes there for afternoon coffee."

She nodded.

"How many beds here?"

"Around eight hundred. Though many of those are on the lower floors. It seems that they had control of it for a few days after the incident in Alpine but then there was a breach and the colonel decided to lock down access to any of the levels below the fourth floor. Level four is the main operations for the military. You won't find anyone else down there except them. They have turned it into their own barracks with sleeping quarters, offices, a firing range, storage of supplies. I've heard there is an armory down there filled with M4s, and all manner of shit. I'd love to get my hands on that. Anyway, they work in shifts. Never the same face in an eight-hour window."

"How many?" she asked.

"What?" Lars asked.

"Soldiers."

"Around thirty, give or take. It's hard to tell but there's enough of them to provide around-the-clock protection to all of us up here while the doctors conduct business. Most are posted at the stairwells on each level, a couple roof-side and the rest are watching over the doctors and nurses."

"Got to keep them alive," Sergio said sarcastically as they continued going down to level six. "Level five is used for regular day-to-day medical attention for anyone that has clearance to this building. Level six is common room, cafeteria, administration offices, and that's where Lynch is usually stationed."

"Do you see her often?"

"Not that much. She comes and goes. When she's around the Chinook is topside. That's why it wasn't there a moment ago. She's probably headed off to the FEMA camp or to find new test subjects."

"But she already has me."

"Not immune. You're not the only one they are testing on. They are testing the infected, trying to reverse the process using whatever samples they are taking from you. When they don't make it, they have to keep heading out to get more."

"Why not just take a few from the ground floor?"

“Too risky. They won’t open up the stairwell, or elevator,” Lars said. “They’ve closed off these levels. They want to keep it airtight. No one gets up here without clearance.”

“How many people above the fourth level?”

Sergio chuckled. “Why so many questions?”

“For five days I’ve seen only two rooms. Call it curiosity,” Jenna said. The fact was it was the not knowing that had driven her mad. Constantly going back and forth between her room and the area where they ran tests was enough to send anyone over the edge. Sergio smirked as they arrived at the common room. It was a large rectangular space with small soft chairs scattered throughout and around twenty tables with hard chairs. At the far end was a canteen which provided drinks and food. A couple of doctors and nurses, as well as a few soldiers, were lined up with plates. They glanced at them as they walked in and one of the nurses whispered into the ear of another.

As she followed Lars to the back of the line, Jenna

became aware that there were eyes on her. "Why are they looking at me?"

"Oh that. You've made a name for yourself around here. Yeah, seems like you're the great hope. Why do you think these people keep working here? Believe me, it's not for the food. You'll see that in a second."

They shuffled along in the line until they made it to the counter.

"What can I get you?"

"I'm thinking lobster, a side of fries followed up with a slice of cheesecake," Sergio said tapping his paper plate against the counter.

"Yeah, right," the broody-looking middle-aged woman said. "We've got chicken and rice, or beef and rice, which one do you want?"

"The one that least tastes like leather."

She dumped an MRI package in front of him and said, "Next."

Sergio shook his head and moved on to the area where they were serving drinks. Lars got his food and moved on and then it was Jenna's turn. She smiled and the lady's expression changed. It was like she was a celebrity or something. The woman nudged her co-worker who had her back turned. "Judith. Look what we got."

Her blond pal turned and stood there, mouth agape.

"What can I get you, hon?"

"Chicken and rice sounds good."

"You got it." She turned and grabbed up a packet and then held up a finger. "Just give me a second, I've got something else that I think you will appreciate." She returned with a buttered roll, and a candy bar. "It's not much and don't tell anyone I gave it to you, otherwise we'll have a war on our hands, but it's just mine and Judith's way of saying thanks."

"For?"

"You know." They nodded and winked.

Jenna frowned, then smiled and thanked them before moving on to get some coffee. Once she collected plastic cutlery, she threaded her way around tables and then took a seat with Lars and Sergio. "Here, you want this?" She threw the bread over to Lars and his eyes widened.

"What the heck."

"Don't show it."

"Where did you get that?" Sergio asked.

"From the two ladies."

"Huh. You're more valuable than I realized. Here, Lars, give me some of that."

"No, it's mine."

"Seriously. You want to do this here?" Sergio asked.

He groaned and broke off half and handed it to him. Both of them stuffed it into their pockets like hungry orphans. Sergio took a spoonful of his MRI and then stared at Jenna.

"What?" she asked as she began to tuck into the food. It wasn't bad. Actually it was better than the crap they were giving her which had expired.

Sergio shook his fork at her. "You're a valuable commodity around here."

"Seems so."

"Is it true, you can't get infected?"

"It appears that way," she said with a mouthful of food. She guzzled it down fast just in case someone came to collect her for more tests and took it away.

"You want to get out of here?"

She nodded. "I want to find my family."

Sergio leaned over his food and eyed the soldiers at the entrance. "I think we can get out but it's not going to be easy. There is a chance we might not make it."

"How?"

"Yeah, how?" Lars asked. Obviously he hadn't discussed this with his pal.

"You leave that to me. For now, just keep your head down, do as they say. Things are a little too hot right now. They are watching. Once they see you're not a threat and not liable to fly the coop they'll back off. I need to check a few things before we move but just be ready. When I say it's time, don't hesitate, don't question me. You move, and you go where I say. You understand?" Sergio said.

She nodded.

Lars looked confused. "You want to fill me in?"

Sergio took another scoop of food and leaned back in his chair. "Nope."

Lars replied, "Great. Just like before."

"This is nothing like before."

"What happened before?" Jenna asked.

"Nothing," Sergio snapped. He got this menacing look in his eyes.

They continued to eat in silence. Twenty minutes later, Colonel Lynch walked into the room with a soldier either side of her. She stopped and looked around and smiled before walking over. Jenna immediately felt a wave of anger.

"Jenna. I hope the new environment is to your liking?"

She shrugged.

"Do you mind?" she asked pointing to a seat. Before Jenna could say no, Lynch took a seat. "Did you show her the outside?" she asked Lars.

"We did."

Lynch turned to Jenna. "Now you can appreciate the

gravity of the situation. What we are doing here can turn back the tide out there. I know you and I haven't seen eye to eye since we've met but I was hoping that would change over the coming weeks. You'll see I'm very much like you, Jenna. I'm married."

"I'm separated," Jenna said. She wasn't proud of it but she didn't want to give Lynch any sense that they were on the same page.

"Oh, that's too bad."

"Not as bad as leaving my son back in Marfa. Not as bad as wondering if they are dead or alive. Not as bad as wiping two towns off the map."

Lynch cocked her head and then she smiled. "Sorenson."

"Yeah, he made it pretty clear before he died what you had in mind." Jenna eyed her. "I hope you sleep well at night." The colonel leaned back in her seat. "I do. I don't lose one minute of sleep. You might not understand what I am doing here but it is for the good of this nation. One day you will thank me for it."

Chapter 7

Neither one spoke about what happened at the motel when they arrived which suited Nick fine. Although his father was concerned about their new guest, Mia, he appeared more worried about another attack and had them load into the Humvee and head out within minutes of arriving. Emerick was perplexed to say the least. Out of all their group he'd been the one to try and get answers but both Brody and Gottman refused to answer. Callie just shook her head when Emerick asked her. It was like they were all privy to some dark secret.

The remainder of the journey took them just over four more days and it might have been longer had they stayed with the Humvee. That thing was a gas guzzler so they swapped it out for an old 4 x 4 Ford truck that still had keys inside. Fortune or fate? Jasper spent an hour discussing the chances of them all meeting and surviving. Most just tuned him out and tried to get some shut-eye but not Nick. He'd given it a lot of thought. Was this meant to happen? What were the odds? And why did some people die when others lived? There appeared to be no reason for bad things happening before the outbreak, did there need to be one now?

The only reasons they stopped on the way to Chicago after that was to fill up with gasoline, or take a leak. On the few times Nick got out to stretch his legs, the view was always the same — desolation. Fires burned out of control, homes lay in ruin, and entire towns were reduced to rubble. Emerick was convinced it had been destroyed by the military. Who else could have had enough firepower to level entire homes? It didn't matter. It was gone and so were the supplies and people. Who knew how many were dead among the debris?

They arrived in the vicinity of Chicago just after eight at night. The concrete city loomed overhead, shrouded by darkness except for a few small pockets of light that lit up the night. Were they fires started on purpose or due to a city out of control? The closer they got to the city the harder it was to slalom around vehicles. Eventually they had to leave behind the truck and go the rest of the way on foot due to a long line of vehicles, many that had crashed into each other. It had to have been the biggest pileup in history. Like dominoes one after the other they had slammed into the back of the next. But that wasn't the real eye-opener. It was what was on the ground. Like litter, bodies were strewn everywhere. They had seen a lot of dead bodies up to that point but the city brought it to a new level.

"Keep your eyes closed," Callie said to Mia. Mia had taken to Callie and wouldn't even look at Nick. The guilt he felt was unbearable. He'd only done what he thought was right in the situation. Had he not killed her father, all three of them could be dead.

It felt like they were the only ones in the world as they traipsed down I-55 with the city in the distance.

"Where is everyone?" Callie said.

"No reason to be out here," Jasper replied. Large billboard signs advertising different businesses had been sprayed over with the words *Turn back now or die.* Was it a joke? Nick figured it had to be as death was everywhere. They had yet to enter a town or city which hadn't been left in ruins or wasn't dangerous.

Nick climbed up onto the bed of a semi-trailer truck that had T-boned into another vehicle. They clambered over and continued on skirting around the dead, and keeping their masks and gloves on.

"Seventy-two hours. This is the result," Emerick said. The soldier who'd helped them back in Alpine had made it clear that the infected wouldn't live past three days. "Hence the reason why so many are dead."

The city itself wasn't quiet. While there were no trucks or vehicles moving around the streets, the sound of gunfire was a constant. Who was shooting who? There was no way to know the danger that lurked inside the city but if the rumors about gangs in Chicago were true, they could be signing their death warrant.

"You do know where you're going, right?" Devan asked Brody as he marched forward while Gottman who was now walking without a crutch tried to keep up.

"Sorenson said the CDC."

"Which is where?"

"No idea," Brody said.

"Are you kidding?" Emerick chimed in. "We've come all this way and you don't even know where the damn building is?"

"We'll find it."

"Oh sure we will, let me just pull out my GPS." He pulled out his phone. "Ah, that's right the internet and phone service went down over a week ago." Emerick scoffed.

"Put a sock in it," Chad said. "We'll find the place."

"I'm sure we will. I'm just hoping it's before we walk into the wrong neighborhood." He brought up a pair of night vision binoculars he'd grabbed from a store in one of the first towns they'd entered upon leaving Alpine. Had they not been among the first to know about the outbreak, Nick was sure the store wouldn't have had half as many survival tools and supplies in place.

Nick glanced at Mia. She scowled at him and refused to speak when he asked her a question so he'd stopped trying days ago. Besides the few times she replied to Callie she didn't say a word. Trauma. PTSD, his father said. Even though she hadn't witnessed her father's demise, she would have heard it. It was common for those who'd lost someone to shrink back into a shell and not reemerge for months, even years. How much more would a ten-year-old do so?

"I think we should bed down for the night," Chad said. "It will be easier to find the place in the morning. Besides, I'm starving. We need to find food ASAP."

His father agreed.

"Where does one bed down for the night in an apocalypse?" Emerick asked with a smirk on his face. He knew full well but looked as if he was wanting to wind up Chad. Chad didn't respond.

All of them moved quietly looking up at the tall buildings. Nick had a sense someone was watching. He was well aware that someone might take a shot at them if they were spotted. No one stood around waiting for confirmation if a person was infected or not. It was kill or be killed, and with a group of their size it would be easy to take down a few of them before they could react.

"We should probably stay close to the buildings," Chad said motioning for the others to follow.

"Is that how you avoided dying?" Emerick said without looking at him.

"Man, what is your problem?"

"No problem. It's just since we've left Alpine you've been handing out advice as if you think your years in the military qualifies you."

"It does."

"So does hiding and letting your team die qualify?"

"Careful."

"Really?"

Nick's dad piped up. "Emerick. What's the deal?"

"Trust. That's the deal. I don't trust him."

Chad scoffed. "What a guy. I saved your ass in Alpine. I came to your aid in Loraine and here you are still yapping about how I haven't earned trust. We're the ones that..."

Multiple rounds rang out and all of them hit the ground, then scrambled for cover. "You see where that came from?" Gottman asked pressing his back to the wall and taking a peek out.

Brody shook his head then turned to the rest of them. "Everyone okay?"

Under the light of the moon, Callie lifted her hand and it was covered in blood.

"Callie!" Nick said hurrying over. That's when he realized it wasn't her that was hit. It was Mia. One clean shot to the chest. A look of shock was fixed on her face. Callie tried to stem the bleeding while Nick's father hurried over to try and help but it was too late. Within seconds her eyes closed and she breathed her last.

"Shit!" Nick bellowed. He was carrying enough guilt as it was but now he felt equally responsible for her. Had he not brought her, maybe she wouldn't be dead. But then again leaving her behind wasn't an option. The young and the old were the weakest, and in a city where fear ruled, it was only a matter of time before she found herself caught in the crossfire. He didn't believe for a minute someone had targeted her. No one could be that heartless. A few more rounds erupted, bullets ricocheted off the tops of parked vehicles before Nick turned and hurried over to where Chad was. He was trying to get a bead on their attackers. "You see them?"

"No idea. People are damn near invisible in a city this big. And forget using sound. Too many gunshots ringing out." It was true. It felt like they'd walked into a war zone. Every few seconds, they would hear gunfire, some distant, but much of it nearby. Still, rounds kept coming which meant whoever was at fault was out there, nearby and prepared to die if need be. Against his better judgment, Nick broke away from the group, dashing across the road.

"Nick!" his father yelled but he ignored it, rage overwhelming him. He took cover behind a vehicle on the other side of the road and looked back. His father looked pissed. Bad decision-making? Probably, but if they remained together as a group, they were no better than sitting ducks. The shooters were likely scrambling to get into another position. That alone would give the others some advantage or at least a break. Nick darted forward into another position only to see a blur off to his right. He turned to engage but heard the familiar voice of Devan. “Don’t shoot, asshole.”

Devan slammed into him to get some room so he could take cover.

“You want to tell me what you’re playing at? Your father is going apeshit over there.”

“I’ve spotted them.”

“Them?”

“Up there,” he said. “On top of that barbershop.”

Devan took a look. Sure enough there were three individuals with rifles. He pulled back and looked at him. “And?”

“You coming with me?” Nick asked.

Devan frowned. “You have got to be joking. We need

to back out."

"Back out? Back out?" Nick said getting louder. "We just lost..."

"Nick," Devan said cutting him off. "I'm sorry, man. I really am but it's not worth losing our lives over. That whole thing with Mia and her father. You got to let that go. That kind of shit is going to happen a lot more before this is over. Are you going to respond like this every time? Now let's get out of here while we're still breathing."

Nick looked over, frustration gripping him.

Devan grabbed his arm, pointed in the direction of the barbershop and gave a thumbs-up to Brody. A sudden burst of gunfire sent the three ducking for cover. That was their moment to move. They hurried back to the rest of the group and then backed out to the nearest street. Out of view. Out of danger, at least for now, Nick trudged ahead of the group. His father caught up and grabbed him by the arm and swung him around. "You ever pull that shit again, and..."

"And what? Huh? And what, Dad?"

Brody stared at him and looked as if he wanted to say something. Nick tugged his arm out of his father's grip and continued on. He expected his father to let it go but he wouldn't. He fell in step. He didn't say anything at first, then he came out with it. "I can't lose you. I couldn't handle it."

"You seemed to handle it real fine when Will died."

"That was different."

"Not exactly. I was invisible to you then and you seemed okay with it. Just pretend I'm not with the group."

"Don't act like that."

"Like what?"

"Like you think I don't care."

"You don't."

His father placed a hand on his shoulder and stopped him. The rest of the group passed by. Callie looked back, a mix of concern, shock and fear masking her face.

"I might have made a few mistakes."

"A few? You are speaking to the wrong person, Dad.

But maybe if we find mom you can have a heart-to-heart then."

"What happened between me and your mother affected you. I get it. I'm sorry, son. I really am. Like I said back in Alpine."

"I know what you said. You say a lot of things. It's your job to know what to say. Maybe that's why mom left. She knew you would only talk your way out of whatever issue you both had." He dropped his head and sighed. "But here's the thing, Dad, she was looking to see what you would do, not what you would say. And so was I."

With that said Nick continued on past him.

The tension between them had thickened since the divorce. Losing Will had been tough but at least then his father didn't speak to him, or his mother for that matter. He became like a ghost to them, passing them like a ghost ship in the night. The group had walked a fair distance ahead. Nick didn't bother to jog to catch up. He watched Callie and the others disappear around a corner, entering another street.

"You're right," his father said. "I shut you out on purpose."

Nick threw up a hand. "Finally, some truth."

"But it wasn't because I didn't love you. It was because you reminded me of Will."

"Well I'm not Will."

"I know that but you're still my son and…" he trailed off as if lost for words.

"He's been dead a long time, Dad, isn't it time that you put it behind you before it's too late?"

"I'm trying, son. Believe me, I am."

Nick shook his head. He really didn't want to get into it. This was why he chose to live with his mother. He could have stayed with his father when they split six months ago, it certainly would have made it easier to go to school in Marfa, but then he would have had to endure the silent treatment. At least with his mother she acknowledged he was there. His father would just grunt at him. Nick walked around the corner and then stopped, both of them did. Before them were close to twenty armed black guys with bandannas over the lower part of their faces. Chad, Emerick, Callie, Devan and Jasper were all being held at gunpoint.

A black guy stepped forward and dropped his bandanna. His white teeth flashed as he broke into a grin. "Welcome."

Chapter 8

Few words were exchanged as Brody and the others were hustled to a collection of flashy cars akin to something out of *The Fast and the Furious.* Stuffed into a trunk, Brody found himself squeezed into the cramped space with his son. They had no idea of where they were being taken, or if they would be alive by the end of the day, he just knew they were outnumbered, outgunned and in no position to argue.

The engine roared to life, letting out a guttural burp, and they bumped around as the car swerved out of the lot and off down the road at a crazy speed. Brody tried to keep count of how many turns they took, and whether it was left or right, so he could get an idea of where they were, but he lost count after a while. It was as if the driver was purposely going around the block a few times to disorient them, though that could have just been because they were coming under attack. A round speared the trunk a few inches from his face, leaving a gaping hole in the side. Nick's eyes widened and Brody clasped a hand around his neck to reassure him. He was anything but relaxed. His heart thumped in his chest and his stomach roiled with nausea from engine fumes.

"Are they going to kill us?" Nick asked.

"If they wanted to, they already would have," Brody replied. He didn't think death was in the cards for them, at least not yet, but finding themselves rolling around in the back of a gangbanger's car wasn't instilling hope.

As quickly as it began, the car swerved hard to the right, bounced up a curb and screeched to a halt. The engine rumbled, and Brody heard a large truck moving. A few seconds later the car rolled forward, slowly this time. It continued on for a minute or two then stopped. The engine died and two doors slammed. The next moment the trunk was opened and two meaty paws reached in and hauled them out.

Blinding bright lights shone in their eyes. Brody squinted and shielded his face with one hand, and that was when he could see where the light was coming from. The vehicle they were in had turned and joined the others to form a circle. All the headlights, along with some from a truck, shone down on them. Brody and the others were thrown on their knees in the middle of the circle and told to wait.

"You okay, chief?" Gottman asked.

"I think we are beyond the point of calling me chief, Gottman."

He nodded and smiled. "Shit just keeps getting better, doesn't it?"

"Well I think I would rather have taken on those fools back in Loraine than these guys," Brody said. The twenty they had seen had multiplied. There had to have been more than sixty at a rough head count and that was just in his immediate view. Some were sitting on top of the cars, others hanging out of the driver's side windows, and the rest leaning against the hoods with handguns and AR-15s in hand. All were dressed in black with large gold chains hanging around their necks.

Suddenly a gun went off, and the chatter ceased.

From between two vehicles, a large, tall black guy emerged with one hell of an afro, and sporting a pair of aviator shades — an odd choice being as it was night. Around his neck was a collection of brown beads and a large cross. In his right hand was a wood staff, the kind that Gandalf might have been accustomed to wield, though shorter. He banged it against the ground as he walked forward and the rest of the men let out a chant.

"Welcome. Welcome. I'm Malik. Now what have we got here? Two cops. But not from around here," he said walking up to Gottman and tearing the patch off his left sleeve. He gazed at it closely. "Alpine, Texas." He crouched down and looked at them both. "You two are a long way from home. What brings you here?"

"I'm trying to find my wife," Brody replied.

"Is that so? On vacation was she when the shit hit the fan? Or did she hook up with another man and you're here to settle a score?"

"Neither."

"Then where's your wedding band?"

"I took it off."

He laughed and stood up. "He took it off. Only two reasons a man takes off his band. He's either getting a bit of ass, or he's tired of the ass he's getting. Which is it for you?"

"Neither."

The guy brought the tip of his staff to Brody's chin and forced it up. "You know, cops around here don't last long."

"I ain't a cop."

"No?" He laughed. "So you just fancy yourself as one…Chief Jackson," he said pointing to his nametag on his breast pocket with his staff.

"I meant to say, I was a cop, I'm not now."

"Oh, how quickly the snake sheds his skin."

"Look, man, can we cut the crap? Where the hell are we?" Emerick piped up.

The guy chuckled and looked his way. "Ah, a wise ass. I like that." He walked along the line of them and stopped in front of Emerick. “And you are?”

“Emerick Jones.”

“Well Emerick Jones. You are in Washington Square, aka our turf. And you walked right into it. I hope for a good reason.” He walked away from him and returned to standing in front of Brody. “So where is this wife of yours?”

“At the CDC, the military took her.”

“Huh. She wouldn’t have anything to do with this outbreak, would she?” he asked, leaning back against a car and taking out of his top pocket a joint. One of his guys stepped forward and flicked open a Zippo lighter. A flame flickered as he took a few strong puffs and then blew the rest out the corner of his mouth.

“No, but the military do,” Chad answered before Brody could.

“And you would know, hey, soldier boy?” He got up and walked over to him. “I’ve gotta say. You really are a strange group. I’ve seen my share of gangs roaming the streets, lost tourists and locals but you guys…” He took another hit and crouched in front of Chad to blow it in his face. "You are something else."

The group around him started laughing. "But you know what. I kind of like that. I'm interested to hear more. In fact that's the only reason you're not dead right now." Gone was the joking look, he tossed his staff to one of his pals and pulled out a Sig Sauer and placed it up to the head of Chad. "I hate cops but soldiers, they've moved right up above them. Now give me one reason not to blow your fucking brains out right now."

Brody tried to intervene but Malik told him to shut up.

"No, let's hear from the soldier boy."

"There are immunes. His wife is one."

"Is that so?" He removed the gun from his temple and looked to his right where he gave a nod to one of his men. They broke away and Malik returned to Brody. "Well why didn't you say so?" He slid the handgun back into the small of his back and helped Brody to his feet. He let out a whistle and several of the guys jumped into the vehicles and reversed back giving them a better view of where they were.

"Come. Tonight you will eat with us. Tomorrow I'll take you to the CDC."

He put an arm around Brody as if he was a good friend and guided him forward towards a Burger King. Malik could see him frowning. He began to laugh. "Yes. It works. The power might be out but we have enough generators and gas to keep what we need here going." He pointed to some of the buildings dotted around the lot filled with souped-up cars. There was a Walmart, Rent-A-Center, Dollar Tree, thrift store, spa, auto parts shop and many more stores. They had taken over the entire block. The main streets into the square were blocked off by large eighteen-wheeler trucks. "Of course if you would prefer Chinese, we have that too," he said pointing to a store that was lit up on the far side of the lot.

"How many of you are there?"

"Gangs?" Malik replied.

"In yours?"

"Over four hundred and sixty-three of us, at my last count. Not everyone is here, most of my guys are out patrolling the streets making sure some of the gangs don't come this way."

"How many gangs?" Gottman asked.

"Estimated at around a hundred thousand members divided between fifty-seven gangs in Chicago," Malik replied. "There are three big areas. You've got the south, west and north side. Most of the gangs are wannabes. They don't stand a chance. Never have. The top dogs are the Gangster Tribe, then you have Gangster Disciples, Latin Kings, La Raza, Black P Stones, Black Disciples, Vice Lords and Four Corner Hustlers. That's just to name a few," Malik said turning his back and pushing into the Burger King. Inside there were about eight gang members tucking into burgers while two were out back whipping up a storm. A generator churned, and the smell of meat was intoxicating. Brody saw his son's face light up, as did everyone's. It had been a while since they'd eaten much more than noodles, canned items, chips and candy bars.

Everything else had either been looted from the stores, or was hard to come by. Of course the greatest stash to be found would be in homes and that's where they'd found theirs. It was easier to find abandoned homes, ones where people had been attacked or fled, than it was to find a full grocery store.

"Hey Trevon. Whip up whatever these guys want, and while you're at it, get me a chocolate milkshake."

Trevon was a huge guy but mostly belly. He towered over the counter and was wearing a white apron and a hairnet. "We have everything we need and what we don't have, we find quite easily," Malik continued.

"And the cops?" Brody asked.

"They showed up after the power went out but we had already locked down this area. On a good day they didn't like coming to our neck of the woods. They soon changed their tune and got the hell out of Dodge when violence erupted in the streets." Malik slumped down into one of the booths and continued to puff on his joint. He offered a hit to Brody but he passed it up. Gottman didn't. He took it and that brought a smile to Malik's face. "Always wondered where all our weed went when they busted a deal."

Gottman squinted and blew out smoke. "Yep, we had a tidy little stash at our department. Most of it gets burned up but the odd baggie disappears." He grinned.

"Anyway, we were already in the area. You could say we lived like rats in the sewers, only coming out when we needed to," he said rubbing his finger and thumb together to indicate business. "I wanted to make sure that places like Walmart, this place, and some of the others weren't looted. So we moved in and set up shop. Blocked off the streets. We have men watching this place around the clock. Some you see, some you won't until it's too late."

"Like until you kill a little girl?" Nick asked, a scowl on his face.

"Did I just catch some attitude?" Malik asked, his smile disappearing.

"Excuse my son. He's a little torn up over someone we lost tonight."

“Yeah, one of us has to be.” Nick said as he turned and walked away.

“Fiery boy you got there.” Malik stared at Nick as he joined the others waiting for their burgers. He turned back to Brody.

“We don’t kill kids. Not young ones that is. Where did happen?”

“Over on the corner of South Western Avenue and 25th. They were positioned above a barbershop.”

“Yeah, that’s not our guys. I know who they are. Sorry for your loss.”

He looked again at Nick before turning back to Brody. “So, tell me more about this wife of yours.”

* * *

“Hey you think I could get mine with cheese? I mean if you have it?” Devan asked bouncing on the balls of his feet. He jabbed Nick in the gut. “So, what do you make of this place? Cool, right? Real food. Man, I miss this. Just smell that.”

“I smell a lot of bullshit.”

"C'mon man. They could have killed us. Now we eat like kings."

"How long do you think this will last?"

"I'm not really thinking like that, Nick," he said leaning forward and taking his bag of food. "And I think you should ease up." Nick grabbed up his bag and they wandered over to a table to join Callie and Jasper who were tucking into their food. Devan slipped in and leaned against the window. "Always wanted to come to Chicago and I've got to say, this place is turning out to be everything and more."

"Devan, we lost someone tonight," Jasper said motioning to Callie who still had tears in her eyes. Devan paused before taking a huge bite of his burger. He chewed a little and looked at her.

"No, I get it. But there is nothing we can do. We've seen people die. Hell, I lost a lot of good friends back in Marfa. I didn't see you weeping for them."

Callie got up and walked away, joining Chad and Emerick at a different table.

"Well done," Nick said, shaking his head.

"What? It's true. Ah, screw you all." He focused on eating and Nick looked out observing Malik's men all over the lot. He didn't like it one bit. Maybe his father, Chad and Gottman trusted this guy but not him.

"You know what's going to happen, right?" Nick said. He pulled out his burger and looked inside it first to make sure they hadn't stuffed it with mind-altering substances, like crack or heroin, or arsenic.

"Do tell," Jasper said.

"We'll lead them to the CDC and find ourselves with a bullet in the back of the head. Mark my words. I say we get out tonight."

"Are you out of your mind?" Devan asked.

"I have to agree with Devan," Jasper said. "It might be the first decent night of sleep we'll get since this whole thing kicked off. At least we don't have to worry about someone slitting our throats in the night."

"You might want to think about that again," Nick said casting a glance over to Malik who was looking at him.

The guy gave him an uneasy feeling. There was something about his demeanor that didn't feel right. That also went for this place. It all seemed a little too good to be true. Nick tucked into his food.

"Well if we die tonight, we die with full bellies," Devan said before cracking up laughing. The guy didn't have a serious bone in his body. Nick only wished he could see the funny side of the situation. The wolves were at their door and to Nick, fattening them up first came hand in hand. He felt like a prisoner on death row having his last meal.

Chapter 9

One day earlier

Sergio was true to his word. He had a plan to escape. He'd been observing the rotation of armed guards throughout the eight days they'd been there. He'd managed to get his hands on a pen and a notepad, and he'd taken notes on a few night shifts doing cleaning so he could get a better feel for the flow and function of the facility. Cleaning required going to all of the floors except the ones below the fourth level. It was the only duty that gave a person access to all of the facility including the parts that were off limits.

They had convened in the common room for what she thought was going to be another chance for Lars to complain about the facility when Sergio pulled out the pen, removed the end and slid out a scrap of paper. He glanced around a few times and kept his back to the soldiers at the door.

"We leave in half an hour."

"What?" Lars spat.

Up until that point he hadn't informed them when they would be leaving but just to be ready when he notified them. To say Jenna was caught off-guard was an understatement. It was one thing to discuss escaping, another to do it. They would only get one shot at it. If they were caught, all privileges would be revoked and she would no doubt find herself back in that cramped room several stories up. That was not in the cards. She couldn't endure that again. That's why she'd begun to question whether an escape attempt was worth it. Sure, she didn't like being a guinea pig for their trials but at least she was getting fed three meals a day, had her own room, her own bathroom and the company of people from her own town. They weren't exactly a joy to be around as Lars complained the whole time and Sergio rarely spoke but it was better than nothing.

Sergio turned the paper around so they could see his sketch. One side showed the different levels, where the soldiers convened, slept and worked, the armory, the elevator shafts and stairwells. The other gave a rundown of the shift rotations, and soldiers' movements on each of the floors. He had it down to a science.

"What are we looking at here?" Lars asked.

"In thirty minutes from now they perform a shift change, soldiers will go up to the fifth floor, a group will go back to the fourth. There is a small window of opportunity. Like five minutes when the elevator shaft here has no one near it, and this stairwell is empty."

"How can you be sure?" Jenna asked.

He scoffed. "It's been that way every day since we've arrived. I hardly think it will change today," he replied before taking a drag of his cigarette and casting a nervous glance over his shoulder. Two guards at the door talked to each other. Nothing was out of the ordinary. That was the key. They were used to seeing the same faces, the same people talking. There were no threats, and where they were sitting was out of view of the camera.

"Okay so how do we do this? They aren't going to let

us just traipse down the stairwell together. You might have access for cleaning duties but that still leaves me and Jenna."

"Hold on a minute before we get to that. You've covered us getting down to the fourth floor but which way is out from there?"

Sergio tapped his finger against the elevator closest to the stairwell.

"You are joking?" Jenna asked. "The elevators aren't working."

"Leave that to me. That's where the next thirty minutes come in. I need you guys to create a distraction."

Lars leaned back in his seat and began shaking his head. "I don't like this. I don't like it one bit. Where are you going to be in this distraction?"

"Making sure the elevator is operational. One of us has to get it going."

Jenna put up a hand. "Even if this worked. You are expecting us to go down to the ground floor where the infected are. I might be immune but you aren't, and even if I am, that doesn't mean I can't be killed. We are dealing with lunatics, people that are unhinged, deranged, completely batshit crazy. How the hell are we meant to protect ourselves?"

"I already have that covered."

"You do?" Lars said. "Well, by all means enlighten us."

"You need to trust me."

"Trust you. What's to say that this isn't all some means of creating a distraction so you can get out and leave us behind?" Lars said.

Sergio tapped ash into a tray and scowled. "Why the hell would I do that?"

"It certainly would make escape easy," Jenna said, backing up Lars.

He pointed his finger at them. "You are both out of your minds. I might be able to get myself out but do you really think I want to be out there…by myself?" He chuckled and looked over his shoulder again. "Like I said, you will have to trust me if you want to get out. You do still want to get out, right?"

Jenna cut Lars a glance and they both nodded.

"Right, then it's settled. Here's what you need to do."

* * *

Lars grumbled after Sergio exited the common room. "He's making us the sacrificial lambs. Why he thinks this will work is beyond me."

"It's not going to work," Jenna said. "I'm afraid your friend has thrown you to the wolves. You were right, Lars. He wants to get out and we are the distraction."

"I knew it. He made me feel like I was crazy for even suggesting it but why would I expect anything else from him after what happened in Alpine."

Jenna frowned. "What happened? What do you mean?"

Lars' expression changed and he went red in the cheeks. "Um. It's nothing. Look, what do we do?"

"We adjust the plan. It can't be us causing the argument. They'll take us in with them. Give me a minute, just be ready to leave immediately. We won't have long." Jenna got up with her plate and went to the back of the line for more food. It rarely occurred. People didn't get seconds in this place. While they had enough supplies in the hospital to last them several months, they still had to be careful. As there were already too many mouths to feed. She'd seen the ones who'd tried it. Those who were worked hard and made to feel like it was a privilege to be there by Lynch. In some ways Lynch was right, it was better than being out there but hiding behind walls and soldiers would only last so long. In the short time Jenna had been there she'd heard rumors swirling. She wasn't the only one unsatisfied with the status quo. Being cooped up twenty-four hours a day, being followed around by soldiers and made to eat the bare minimum only stretched so far. One of these people was an orderly by the name of James Whitefield. A large man whose mere presence put the soldiers on edge, he had already voiced his complaints to Judith, the lady behind the counter serving. Only two days ago he'd kicked up a fuss and slammed his tray down demanding more after he was served up half of his usual serving. Fortunately, Judith was able to deescalate the situation before the soldiers moved in. Jenna saw him across the room, seated with a few others. He was once again complaining about the place. She planned to use that to her advantage.

Jenna looked over at Lars who was leaning back in his seat.

"Hi Judith," Jenna said as she reached the front of the line.

"Back again, are we."

"I hate to ask as I know the rules but I was wondering if you might be able to make an exception, just this one time. For some reason I'm more hungry than usual. I'm guessing it's all those tests they've been running on me. It really takes it out of you. You know?"

Judith grimaced and looked at the soldiers. "I don't know. I would like to but…"

"Ah, it's okay. By the way, it looks like they might have found a formula for the cure. I'm going today to have one final test. But they're confident they've managed to stabilize the PH levels and reverse the disease."

Judith's eyes widened. "Really? Wow, that's wonderful news. Well. I mean, if they are on the verge of a breakthrough, that's cause for celebration, right? Look, I think we can see our way to finding you something extra." She turned and disappeared below the counter and emerged with some milk and a packet of cookies, and then she filled Jenna's plate with some more potatoes, soup and an extra bun. "How's that?"

"Perfect. Thanks kindly, Judith."

"Oh no, it should be us thanking you."

Jenna turned with a smile on her face. She walked away and threaded around tables until arriving at James' table. She looked back over her shoulder and saw that Judith was busy helping the next person in line. "James. You hungry?"

"Always. When are we not?"

"Good. I'm not that hungry today, I thought you might be able to have my seconds." She clearly emphasized the word *seconds* before placing the tray in front of him in full view of the other three around the table. All of their jaws went slack.

"Seconds? They dished you up seconds?"

"Yeah, they've been doing it for some time. I guess because I hold the key to the cure. But hey, don't get bothered by it. You can have mine."

"Well, I really appreciate that, Jenna. But…" he trailed off and looked towards Judith and the other server. A scowl formed on his face. He was falling for it hook, line and sinker.

"And what about us?" the other three protested. "Don't we get seconds?"

"You get your own," James said wrapping his mammoth arms around the tray to prevent them snatching any of the items. Jenna patted James on the shoulder and winked at him before turning and strolling back to Lars who had a look of confusion on his face.

She sat down across from him and he grinned. "What are you up to, Jenna?"

"Just wait for it."

Both of them watched as one of the men tried to

snatch the cookies unsuccessfully. A dispute arose between the men but instead of the others attempting to take on the brawny orderly, they got up and made their way to the front of the line to request seconds themselves. Of course, Judith turned them down and sent them on their way but not before a soldier came over and told them to settle down or they'd be removed. That wasn't the end of it. They returned to the table and thought they would try a second time to take from James.

"Come on. Share what you have. You aren't even meant to have that," a voice bellowed as a man stood to his feet. A look of anger spread across James' face. As he rose to confront the man the other two guys grabbed food from his tray. James reacted by grabbing one of them by the collar and yanking him across the table.

From there it just spiraled down.

The two soldiers left their post and ran towards the men to break it up.

"That's our cue. Let's go!" she said rising and ducking out before they had the chance to realize they were gone.

They hurried down the corridor and slipped into the stairwell making their way down to level four. The sound of their boots echoed. Jenna's pulse sped up at the thought of running into a soldier. What would they say? It was made clear to everyone that level four was off limits. There was no reason for anyone but soldiers to go down there. Only one other person had tried to find a way out and they were now confined and had many of their privileges taken away.

Jenna glanced at her watch. The only thing they were following in Sergio's schedule was the timing and they were only two minutes out. Lars pulled back the door and peered into the corridor on the fourth floor. The sound of chatter further down could be heard. There was a room two doors down that was used to hold cleaning supplies. Sergio said he would be waiting there.

"You ready?" Lars said. Jenna nodded and they rushed out, their feet pounding the floor until they burst into the room. Sure enough, there he was, sitting on an overturned bucket, smoking a cigarette.

"You're off by two minutes."

"We had a little trouble," Jenna said.

With that said Sergio rose and went to the door and peered out.

"Did you manage to get the elevators working again?"

"Yes and no."

"What does that mean?" Lars asked.

"You're just going to have to follow my lead. But understand this, hesitation will cause all of this to fail. From here on out you must do as I say. Do I make myself clear?"

"Why do I not like the sound of that?" Jenna said.

He paused at the door then flung it open and rushed towards the elevator. They followed him, hearts pounding, sweat beginning to trickle down Jenna's face. Sergio inserted a key into a hole and twisted it, and the elevator shaft door opened, except there was no elevator, just cables going down into darkness.

"Where's the elevator, Sergio?"

He pulled out of his pocket rags and without

answering him tossed a couple to each of them. "Wrap them around your hands and slide down. It will prevent the metal cutting them open."

Lars opened his mouth, and said, "I'm—"

Sergio was quick to cut him off. "I told you. You want out. Follow me."

With that said he dived off the edge into the blackness and the sound of cabling whipping around could be heard and then him sliding down. Lars looked at Jenna and shrugged before doing the same. As soon as he was gone, Jenna peered over but not before looking both ways down the corridor. She could hear someone approaching. She wrapped the thick cloth around her hands and was just about to leap when a soldier yelled, "Hey. You!"

She cast a glance to her right and saw him beginning to break into a run.

"Don't you do it. Don't!" the soldier yelled as she turned towards the elevator shaft. Not wasting a second, Jenna leapt out into the void, clasped hold of the grease-covered steel cable and slipped down into the abyss.

Chapter 10

Lynch was furious as she pushed her way past a soldier to see the video footage. She leaned against the desk and looked at the screen, watching it all play out before her eyes. "Who was monitoring these?"

"It was a shift change," Lieutenant Mosley said.

"But we always have one person on them at all times."

"Colonel, what can I say? A mistake was made."

"That mistake might cost you your job," she said as she stormed out barking orders. "I want them found and now!" The colonel crossed over to the elevator and peered down. She shone her bright flashlight into the darkness. If they were down there, they were long gone. She gritted her teeth as she reentered the office where they dealt with surveillance. Even though they didn't visit floors one to three, there were cameras set up so they could see potential threats before they happened. The elevator had been shut down from operating. What they hadn't banked on was the doors being opened and someone sliding down the cables.

“Have you found them yet?”

“Not so far,” a young soldier said, flipping through different views of the levels below. Mosley stood by the door as if waiting for his orders.

“What are you still doing here, Mosley?” she asked without looking at him.

“You want us to go down?”

“Well I don’t want you to go up. Of course I do.”

“The last time we sent men down eight died.”

Lynch whirled around to face him, jabbing her finger at the ground. “I don’t care if every man dies as long as she doesn’t. Do you understand?”

Mosley stared back at her blankly then said, “Yes, colonel.”

A soldier hurried into the room. “Colonel, the president is on the line.” She placed a hand on her forehead and sighed. That was all she needed right now. She had nearly forgotten about the conference call. He was wanting an update. Always updates. Were they any closer to finding the cure? How soon could they have it ready? Had they made any advancement? He wanted her to create a miracle and maybe they would have, had this not happened.

"Just make it happen," Lynch said as she passed Mosley. "And I want an update the moment you spot them."

She charged off to her office trying to think what to tell him. There was no way in hell she would drop this bomb on him. He'd have her head for it. She was already struggling to give a reason why the doctors hadn't discovered the cure through their tests, and he was beginning to question their reasons for having the military there at all. With so much occurring across the country, soldiers were valuable and with more of them than civilians on the front lines, more were becoming exposed to the contagion. The risks were high and the window of opportunity to turn back the tide was getting smaller by the day.

Lynch entered and closed the door behind her. She went over to a mirror on the wall and adjusted her fatigues, tucked a strand of dark hair behind her ear and smiled trying to convince herself that everything was okay. It was all going to be fine. Mosley would send a team of his best down and within the hour they would have her back. Once she was back, things were going to change. She'd been a fool to give her more breathing room. She took a seat in front of the open laptop. There before her on one split screen was the president and on the other was the FEMA rep, Margaret Wells.

"Good evening, Colonel Lynch."

She smiled back but didn't say anything.

"It's my unfortunate duty to notify you that the outbreak is now in twenty-three of the fifty states."

Lynch shook her head. "You said there were only six states infected."

"Known," Wells added, coming to the president's defense. "That was all we knew about. We are getting reports from many of the hospitals all over the country."

"My God. What's the plan?" Lynch asked.

"The plan is still the same. We are relying on you to find a cure. That is the only way we turn this around. Every passing day we are seeing a dramatic increase in violence across the nation. Unstable behavior is becoming the norm. We can't allow it to become the norm," the president said. "So please tell me you have good news for us?"

Lynch took a deep breath. "Yes. Yes I do. We think we have managed to isolate the problem and the recent string of tests have been very positive."

"Translated that means?"

"It means we should have a cure ready within the month."

"A month?" the president asked.

"Yes, sir."

"We won't have any states left within the month. At the rate this is spreading we will have no safe zones left. Can't you speed it up?"

"I'm afraid I'm not involved in the process. I simply

look at the reports and speak to the doctors."

"Perhaps we are working with the wrong doctors." The president turned and spoke to one of his Joint Chiefs of Staff and then looked back at the screen. "We will be sending a helicopter to collect the immune. Have her ready to go in the next seventy-two hours."

Lynch's jaw went slack.

"Is there a problem, colonel?"

"No. No problem. Yes, sir. I will have her ready to leave. But um, would you mind sharing where you'll be taking her?"

"Mount Weather. You'll be joining us."

"I will?"

He nodded. The deadpan expression on his face made it clear that it wasn't an invite and they certainly weren't going to meet because he wanted to chit-chat.

She summoned her best smile. "I look forward to it."

At the end of the call, she closed the laptop and sat there staring into space. Seventy-two hours. Three days. That's all she had. She swallowed hard, rose and felt herself become a little dizzy. Lynch gripped the table. She'd stood up too fast. Or maybe it was the lack of sleep. She hadn't been sleeping well, and the constant trips back and forth to FEMA camps were beginning to take their toll. She pulled out her satellite phone and tried to contact her husband. Since the outbreak she had only spoken to him twice. The first was when she informed him that she wouldn't be going on their weekend away, and the second was after Alpine. At that point he said he was safe. She had tried eleven times since then and had only got voicemail. She wasn't sure if he was ignoring her or if he'd succumbed to the outbreak. She rang and once again it went to voicemail.

"Wes. It's me. If you are hearing this. Pick up." There was no response. In times gone by he would cut into her message but not now. "I…wish we had gone away. I wish I had taken your advice and handed in my notice last year. I wish for a lot of things." There was dead air before she said, "I love you. Take care."

With that said she hung up and clutched her phone

tightly before heading back to the surveillance room to get an update.

* * *

They had made it to the second floor. From the moment they'd stepped out of the elevator shaft, fear had gripped Jenna. The walls were smeared with bloody handprints, and several bodies lay in various states of decay. Sergio had handed out N-95 masks and gloves to them but that was the least of her concerns. He'd attempted to get into the armory while doing his cleaning rounds but failed. All of which meant they were unarmed and walking through dangerous territory. The corridor was covered with medical papers, streaks of blood and overturned gurneys. As there was no power, and no generators were powering the lower floors, they were shrouded in darkness. The only light came from what was left of the sun filtering through the windows as it began to set.

"I can't believe you talked me into this," Lars said trudging behind her. Jenna was sandwiched between them as they walked in a line. Without weapons, they'd all taken to picking up anything that could be wielded. Jenna was using a metal pole that looked as if was part of an IV bag stand. Sergio had found a large kitchen knife that was embedded in the back of a dead doctor. Jenna had been the one to wipe it down and clean it off before handing it to him. Lars had peeled back a piece of floor frame, twisted it back and forth and snapped a piece off. It wasn't ideal but it was something at least for now.

"Shut up and keep your eyes peeled," Sergio said.

They hadn't made it but a few yards down the hall when a bearded man burst out of a room and slammed into Sergio, knocking him against the wall. He'd gripped him by the wrist, preventing him from stabbing him, so Jenna swung as hard as she could and took out his legs. As soon as he hit the ground, Lars followed through, driving the metal into his throat. The man gripped his neck as blood gushed out and they moved on.

"Where's the next stairwell?"

"Further down," Sergio said. "By the way, thanks."

"You would have done the same."

The smell of death lingered in the air. Every time they passed another room, they expected to encounter more lunatics. Strangely enough the second floor was clear. At least from what they could tell. Ducking into the stairwell they were greeted by the sight of a man who'd had his head smashed in against the steel railing. His body hung limp, a hand still clutching the bar. They stepped over him and slowly worked their way down. On the first floor they could hear noise.

"This is it. All we need to do is get to the main entrance and we are clear."

"Sounds good in theory. Take a look," Lars said stepping back so Sergio could see what they were dealing with. Jenna got closer and peered under his arm. The first floor was crowded with people, and bodies, hell, she could barely see the waxed floor. It was as if every person in the hospital had decided to attack each other and create a carpet of corpses.

"I'm not going out that way," Lars said closing the

door. “Screw that.”

Sergio threw up a hand. “It’s the only way out.”

“No, it’s not. We can go back up to the second floor, break a window and jump down onto the concrete awning overhanging the main entrance.”

“And you know this because?”

Lars flashed him a confused look as if it was common sense. “I looked over the edge. Look, do you want risk going through that minefield or try it my way?” Lars said as he made his way up the stairs. He’d already made his mind up so Sergio didn’t complain. They followed him and made their way to an area that seemed close to the emergency entrance. Lars pushed his forehead against the window and pointed. “See. There we go.”

Sergio was acting all nonchalant about it. “Whatever.”

Lars turned and looked around and then charged towards a chair. He scooped it up and told them to get out of the way. Jenna moved far back as Lars took a run and tossed the chair as hard as he could at the pane of glass.

Surprisingly it didn't break. It barely cracked. A fine line appeared fissuring out like a spider web.

"What the hell did they make this out of?" Lars asked running his hand over it.

"Get out of the way. Never send a boy to do a man's job," Sergio barked as he picked the chair up and swung it as hard as he could against the glass. Again, the thing didn't break. He tried again. Then again. Each time the chair simply bounced off. Though each time the fissure got larger. It wasn't shatterproof but they had obviously opted for hardened glass.

"Why would they make these so darn strong?"

"Perhaps to withstand tornadoes?" Jenna said.

"Tornadoes?"

"Yeah, Chicago is in Tornado Alley," Jenna said.

"The first I heard."

"It's recent," Jenna replied.

Sergio picked up the chair again. "Would you both shut the hell up?" He scowled and tossed the chair again at the glass. It didn't matter how many times he struck it, only the outer layer of the glass fractured. “Sonofabitch!” Sergio put his hands on his knees and sighed. “I give up. We will have to do this my way,” he said.

“I’m not going down.”

“Then you stay here. I’m done trying to convince you.”

Sergio began trudging towards the door when they heard what sounded like a door closing. “Sergio!” Jenna said in a hushed voice. He’d heard it and stopped in his tracks. He started backing up and all three of them searched for an area to hide. Jenna ducked behind a bench holding surgical scalpels. She reached over and grabbed a scalpel in one hand and kept the metal pole in the other. Out the corner of her eye she saw Lars take up position behind a tall set of trays that were filled with medical devices. She had no idea where Sergio went. They waited there in the silence, hearing footsteps getting closer, then they heard breathing. If it wasn’t for it being night, and the power being off, she was sure they would have been seen.

It felt like a minute passed but it was probably only seconds before the person walked away. Jenna dared to look around the bench. There was no one there. She made a gesture to Lars by putting up two fingers to her eyes and pointing. He stepped out and in a low voice told her to wait. From her concealed position, Jenna watched as Lars ventured out into the darkness. Fear gripped her as she waited. At first she heard him moving, then stillness. Nothing. Not a sound. "Lars?" she said in a whisper. No response. She twisted from a seated position to sneak a peek around the bench. Just as she did it, she felt a hand clasp her shoulder. Before she could let out a cry, fingers wrapped around her mouth. Staring back at her was Lars. He put a finger up to his lips, and made a hush sound. Following that he pointed, and raised three fingers. Her eyes bulged.

A second later, Sergio shuffled around the bench, keeping really low.

He held the knife in his hand and all three of them froze at the sound of several people entering the room.

Chapter 11

The last video footage showed them reentering the second floor, then they went out of view. The cameras were only set up in certain areas, and because each floor was a maze of rooms and corridors, and there was no power on, it was anyone's guess where they were. Colonel Lynch didn't have the nerve to do the hard work, but this was what Mosley thrived on. He and a small team of four soldiers had rappelled down the elevator shaft in pursuit. Now with their night vision goggles on they were clearing each of the rooms while at the same time trying to be as silent as possible. It had been a while since he'd been down there and faced those lunatics. He'd lost many good men at the hands of the deranged. Masked up, the team moved quickly from room to room.

"Clear," he heard Thompson say over the mic.

Mosley looked up at the camera that had given them the last sighting. Lynch was probably watching them, cursing under her breath. The woman had no backbone. Oh, she could bark out orders and order him around like a peasant but when push came to shove, she wouldn't step down off that high horse and get her hands dirty. No, that was left for guys like him. In his long years in the military, Mosley had risen through the ranks by proving himself a valuable soldier of the United States at every turn. He was the last of a dying breed. A warrior. A man who knew he would one day die in his boots but saw that as an honor. His body was full of scars, each one told a story, a fight, a battle waged, and only a select few knew what it had cost him. He'd seen his closest friends, guys that he'd been through boot camp with, have their limbs blown off; he'd cradled guys as young as nineteen as they took their last breath; and he'd charged forward when bullets fell like rain. Fear was never an option in his book. He felt it but he wasn't dominated by it.

"Lieutenant, we have three in our sights."

Mosley got on to Lynch. "We have them."

"Proceed with caution. Take them in."

"Move forward. Do not fire. I repeat. Do not fire."

Two of his team went to one side of the cramped corridor, he and the other two covered the other side. They navigated around the debris and junk clogging up the way ahead. They were within twenty yards of the three when the boots of one of his men struck a metal pole. It rolled and clattered against the wall.

Instantly it caught the attention of the three. Peering through the night vision goggles, it was hard to distinguish if it was them or not. One of them looked like a woman, the other two men. The three charged forward.

"Stop!" Mosley yelled.

A round was fired at his team, and in that instant his men engaged, unloading rapid fire in self-defense.

* * *

"Let's go!" Sergio said as the sound of gunfire erupted. Jenna didn't hesitate, she clasped Lars' hand as Sergio led them out of the room, across the corridor and back into the stairwell. For a brief moment she glimpsed someone collapsing to the ground near the corner of the corridor.

It all happened so quickly. Within seconds they were descending the steps heading for the first floor. This time there was no delay, no hesitation or time to think about the consequences. They hurried into the first floor, stepping on dead bodies as they went. Bone crunched beneath them as they stood on fingers, skin gave way making it feel like they were running across shifting sands.

A figure darted out from the left, and Sergio lunged forward driving a knife into the stranger's chest. "Keep going!" he said as he took a second to retrieve it. In the darkened corridor it was hard to tell whether it was women or men running at them. All Jenna heard was a cry and then the sound of Lars plowing into them. Jenna came to his aid swinging the steel pole like a baseball bat and crushing someone's face. There was no time to wonder if these people were infected or reacting out of fear of them being infected. The war they were fighting was driven by fear on both sides.

Sergio came running up the rear, and she heard a gun

open fire. That's when she saw that he had a handgun and had just taken out two more who had come up the rear and were nearly upon her. Adrenaline pumped through her body as one by one the deranged emerged from darkened corners, some saying nothing, others letting out a wail, all responding with violence.

Jenna screamed as someone sliced her arm with a knife.

Her fear soon turned to anger and her will to survive kicked in. She used every limb she had to fight her way forward, hacking, kicking, punching her way to freedom. Had it not been for Sergio having a handgun, she was certain they would have died in that corridor, overwhelmed by the multiple, back-to-back attacks.

They burst into the main lobby, and saw multiple soldiers dead with rifles beside them. Jenna scooped one up and without any idea of how to shoot one, placed her finger on the trigger and hoped to God it would work. It did. As four lunatics rushed forward, she squeezed and round after round erupted taking them down. To her left,

Lars and Sergio were engaging with more as they pushed forward towards the exit, a revolving door. All the glass at the front of the building was gone, nothing more than shattered pieces on the ground.

"Jenna!" a voice yelled. She turned and saw a cluster of individuals moving down a corridor towards the lobby. Red strobe lights coming off rifles crossed and bounced off walls and floors as they hurried. Sergio pushed her on towards the opening as more patients appeared off to the left, pushing through double doors. Jenna inhaled the cold air as they emerged into the driveway at the front of the emergency area. Vehicles parked haphazardly with doors left open and drivers slumped over wheels, came into view. Many of the dead looked as if they had been fleeing on foot and had been attacked. Dry blood pooled in areas, the sidewalks had streams of red beside them. Shock bore down on Jenna. A colossal weight that made it hard to breathe. The city had turned into a war zone where bodies were left to rot. They only saw one ambulance as they hurried away, and it was empty. There were no medics inside, no patients, and the gurney had been yanked out. Blood covered the inside, and left no question to the fate of those inside.

The sound of gunfire erupted behind them.

"Who was that?" Lars asked Jenna.

"The military."

Sergio led them on, crossing a street and ducking into a heavily forested area of the surrounding park.

Chapter 12

Hours Later.

Nick pawed at his eyes as he awoke. The smell of coffee hung in the air, and the quiet sound of chatter brought the world back into focus. That night they'd slept on living room furniture in Walmart. Located in the heart of Washington Square, the large brown store crouched at the corner of Rockwell and 23rd Street. The inside was one of many stores that were being used in the area for living quarters, like a large-scale home. Boxes had been ripped apart, and furniture had been spread out to give the place a sense of home. If only the owners could have seen it. He rolled off the sofa full of cushions and tossed the blanket to one side. Nick stretched out and yawned looking around at the others. His father, Chad and Emerick were already up and chatting with Malik while Jasper and Callie were still sleeping. He didn't sleep much that night, mainly because he wasn't sure if one of the gang members was going to slit his throat or not. The fact that they were trusting these guys was a tough pill to swallow.

Devan walked over with two cups in hand.

"Is that mine?" Nick asked.

"Hell no, this is for Callie."

Nick frowned but didn't give it another thought. He walked over to a table that had been set up with muffins and coffee. As he poured himself one, Malik slid up beside him. "Your father has quite the story. Is it true?"

"Why are you asking me?"

"Because you know him and I'm sure you don't want any harm coming to him."

Nick turned and looked him in the eye. "Is that a threat?"

Malik smiled and filled up a cup with coffee. He replied without looking at him, "I've been on this planet forty-two years, Nick, I've never once threatened anyone. But that's not to say I haven't done bad things to those who don't listen."

There was no mystery to what he was saying.

"In that case, yes. Yeah, it's true. My mother is immune to the disease. At least that's what they told her. Whether that's true is to be determined."

Malik lifted his shirt and flashed the butt of his handgun.

"Is that meant to scare me?" Nick asked.

Malik's lip curled up.

Nick went to walk away and Malik caught a hold of his arm. "I know you don't trust us. I wouldn't expect you to but we live by a different code out here. It's kill or be killed. Long before this outbreak started, we were living each day as our last. This is no different. For you. Yeah. For us, it's just another day. You'd be wise to know when to speak and when not."

"Can I go?" Nick asked looking at his hand.

"Let's hope you and your father are right."

With that said he released his grip and Nick walked back to the sofa. Callie was now up and nursing a cup of coffee. She and Devan had been watching it all play out. As soon as he approached, Devan wanted the skinny. "So? What's his deal? What did he want?"

"He wanted to know the barber who cut your hair."

"Really?" Devan said running a hand over it and looking over at Malik.

"Oh yeah, the guy digs it."

Devan got up. "I should probably go speak with him."

"Yeah, you do that."

As he walked off, Nick chuckled and took a seat beside Callie.

"He didn't say that, did he?"

"No, but it gives us a moment to chat." He nudged her and she smiled. "Look, um, about today. This might not go our way. If things go south, head east for Maine. I was listening to the radio last night and there is a signal being broadcast about a safe zone on Mount Desert. It's an island just off the coast, close to Ellsworth. I'm not sure how many are there, but they said they have resources and so far have prevented any of the infected from getting onto the island."

"You say that as if you expect it to go wrong. Do you know something we don't? Is that what Malik was talking to you about? Did he threaten you?"

Nick glanced at the ground. "It doesn't matter what he said or where we are. Every day it gets worse out there. There are no guarantees of another tomorrow. We need to realize that and…"

"Nick, you're worrying me."

He smiled and placed a hand on hers. Touching her like that for the first time sent a shiver over him. She'd been a girl he admired from afar for a long time. It seemed almost ironic that when they finally got some alone time, it would be under these circumstances.

"Forget it. Let's get some breakfast."

* * *

Brody stood over the urinal peeing when the door opened and Gottman came in. "Who would have thought we would be peeing in a urinal, inside Walmart, in the great city of Chicago!" He almost sounded elated. Like he'd checked off one of his bucket list items. Brody zipped up and tried washing his hands but no water came out.

"Great."

"They have electricity because of the generators but the water stopped a few days ago. At least that's what Malik said. They have a washroom further down that is set up with tubs full of water for cleaning. As long as you're happy using day-old water from the river. And who knows who's bathed in it, or taken a piss in it for that matter."

Brody glanced at him and Gottman shrugged. "Well it's true."

"You got any of those cigarettes left?"

"No, I'm all out, but I thought you quit?"

"I did. I'm thinking of starting up again."

Gottman chuckled then got this serious look on his face. "You don't trust him. Malik, I mean," Gottman said.

"Do you?"

"Not as far as I could throw him. He'll probably turn on us the moment he gets his grubby hands on your wife."

"My thoughts exactly."

Gottman shook out and zipped up, then proceeded to check each of the stalls to make sure no one was listening in. The last one was locked. Gottman got on the ground and could see a pair of feet. In a hushed voice he said, "Look, it's a two-edged sword. At first, I was against the idea of them coming along but at the end of the day if the military is at the CDC, we're going to need a way in. In some ways we need his crew." Gottman walked over to the mirror and ran a hand over his stubbled face that would soon turn into a full beard. "Man, I need a shave."

"Aisle four. Razors and shaving cream," a voice said.

"Emerick?"

"Here and accounted for. You guys really need to be careful what you say." They heard him doing up his belt. When he came out, he said, "Ah, I wouldn't go in there for a few years." Emerick chuckled to himself as he rubbed his hands on his clothes. Brody grimaced. That was one thing that was liable to kill them long before the outbreak did — poor sanitation. Without clean water, a means of purifying it and keeping themselves clean, it wouldn't be long before they contracted some other disease. They were already stinking to high heaven.

Emerick turned and faced them. "Anyway, we are going to die. That's for sure."

"How do you know?"

"I stepped out last night to have a smoke. I overheard two of his guys shooting the breeze. It's meant to happen after arrival at the CDC. Today is plan A. I think it's clear we need a B. So, did you guys have anything in mind or do you want to hear mine?"

"As long as it doesn't involve any of your mad conspiracy theories," Gottman said before laughing.

* * *

Malik was born in the streets, literally. He never knew his father as he was the son of a crack addict of a mother who gave herself to any man willing to pay for her next hit. Thrown into the foster system, he was carted around to different homes until the age of sixteen when he ran away. He'd like to say that they made an effort to track him down but that would be a lie. No one came searching for him. He was just a strain on the system and there was always another kid ready to take his spot in a manila folder.

Those early years had taught him a lot about life. Only the strong survived. No one gave a shit. And if he was ever going to make something of himself, he had to be willing to fight his way to the top. And fight he did. Stealing food, sleeping anywhere he could find a warm bed and running errands for gang members, he soon made connections and earned a name for himself in the streets. He was a reliable asset to those wanting people dead, or drugs sold, and he was a threat to the cops. By the time he was eighteen, he had killed his first cop, fathered three kids through two different women, and gained himself a position as a gang member within the Gangster Tribe.

There were many dangerous gangs he could have joined but in the city of Chicago, the Tribe stood head and shoulders above the rest. You didn't get in without killing a rival gang member. Most who did the act, did it from a distance. A drive-by shooting allowed them to kill without being shot. Not him. He didn't just want to be another face in a gang, he wanted to send a message to rival gangs, and to Torrence Scott, the head of Gangster Tribe at that time — a message that would make it clear that he wasn't going to settle for being just a yes-man. That's why when he made his kill, he didn't just pick any gang member, he picked the leader of the Latin Eagles — Willie "Youngblood" Washington.

Getting to him was no easy feat but even the tightest groups had holes.

The problem with those wanting to join gangs was they were impatient. It was easier to do a drive-by shooting, and get it over, but that wasn't him. He waited, observed from afar. He sniffed around the Latin Eagles and sought out a weak link. There was always one among a gang. One who was tired of the gang life, one who was being reached out to by a community church, one whose mother hadn't stopped praying for them. All he needed to do was find out who they were, jump them on the way to the community church, and the rest was like taking candy from a baby.

The one that gave up Willie died in the back streets. His blood flowed, a sweet release for someone who wanted out. He got it, it just wasn't the exit he'd imagined.

Within days of finding out where Willie Washington hung out, knowledge only known by his gang members, Malik was able to end his pitiful life. He'd been eating at an Italian spot on the Lower West Side when Malik paid him a visit. It was all about timing. He could recall the adrenaline pumping through his veins as he pulled up a few blocks from the restaurant and pushed a silenced gun into the back of his jeans. The anticipation of killing him was nearly as good as wondering what Torrence would say when he returned with his head. Washington had been a thorn in Torrence's side for years. A constant threat that had caused the deaths of many in the Tribe. Killing him would make Malik stand out when others barely were noticed. Too many faces. Too many wannabe gangsters. The only way to rise through the ranks was to demonstrate no fear.

As he waited for members of his gang to go with him to the CDC, he drifted back to that day in his mind. The anticipation. Sneaking in the back door of the restaurant after killing someone from the kitchen. Waiting in the shadows for Washington to step into the bathroom. The look on his face as he glanced in the mirror as Malik came up behind him with a gun to his head. He could have shot him. The chances of the gun being heard were next to none but that wasn't how he wanted it to end. No, killing him and delivering his head to Torrence was only one part of the equation. Sending shock waves throughout the city was a must. Making it clear that a person could be touched no matter who they were or how big their gang was, was what caused him to film the stabbing of Washington.

Driving the knife into his back and bringing him down was almost too easy. He thought Washington would at least put up a fight. He didn't. He squirmed, struggled, then accepted his fate.

Like a thief in the night he slipped out of there with his head and returned victorious, striding through the midst of hundreds of gang members with a bag dripping with blood. He tossed it before Torrence and dropped to a knee.

Cheers, and laughter erupted before Malik was lifted upon the shoulders of many and carried around like a king. Never before had anyone had the nerve or wits to commit such a brazen act. That one action elevated him into new status. Where it took others years to rise through the ranks and be seen as leadership material, he had managed to do it within one day.

Seven years later he took his rightful position as the leader of the gang.

Since then many had come forward and challenged

him, many had attempted to take his life in the same fashion as he had Washington's, but he was always one step ahead.

"Malik," a voice said in almost a whisper. He turned his head to see Runt. Runt was a small kid who he used as his ears and eyes in the gang. Although most members of the Gangster Tribe were incredibly loyal, he knew a day would come when someone would disagree with his decisions and direction, and would become a turncoat. It wasn't a matter of if, only when. The hope was when that day arrived, Runt would hear about it and Malik would be able to prevent his throat being slit in the night. They all had their reasons for being in the gang. In Runt's case, he had run away from the foster system and was caught picking the pocket of one of Malik's own gang members. Caught as he tried to escape, death would have been his fate, except Malik saw potential in him. Runt reminded him of himself. If he could get close enough to steal from Malik's own guys, what else was he capable of?

"What is it?"

Runt glanced around nervously before leaning in.

"You're not going to like this."

He whispered into his ear and Malik's heart dropped. "Are you sure?"

Runt pulled out a cell phone from his pocket and played back the recorded conversation.

"Thank you, Runt."

Runt was about to walk away when Malik stopped him. "Runt, do me a favor."

"Anything."

* * *

Half an hour later, a large crowd gathered in the heart of Washington Square, a dozen vehicles revved in preparation for heading to the CDC. Malik had considered waiting until he was back from the trip before he did this but timing was everything. He thought he could kill two birds with one stone and he fully intended to do so. Some of his men held AK47s, and others had AR-15s over their shoulder. The atmosphere was alive with music playing, and a few lowrider cars bouncing with the power of hydraulic pumps. The sound of gunfire was always present, near occasionally, distant at all times. It had become the norm. Survivors killing the infected, gang members attacking each other. But it never happened where they were. They had more than enough people to secure a perimeter, and watch over them twenty-four seven.

Malik made his way into a large clearing in the middle of a parking lot just beyond the Walmart. He eyed the group they would lead to the CDC. Malik had mixed views about them — on one hand he admired their courage — walking into the city, seeking out a loved one. Then on the other hand he considered it foolish. But, regardless, if it was true. If there was a cure and a way to turn back the tide of deranged, how valuable would that person be in the right hands? How much would the government pay? Malik wasn't getting any younger and he knew a day would come when someone as hungry as he was would rise through the ranks and set his eyes on leading the group. When that day came he wanted to be ready, ready to disappear, ready to start again afresh, elsewhere. It was his plan B, his exit strategy, everyone needed one. When Torrence Scott handed over the reins, he left Chicago behind. No one knew where he went but a year later Malik had received a postcard from the Bahamas. There was no message but it was signed TS. He liked to think that Torrence was sipping on a beer, running a small gig down by the beach, living out his final days in peace, free from fear, and free from harm.

Malik slammed his staff against the concrete to get everyone's attention.

One of his men fired a round to quiet the rowdy.

"I consider all of you my tribe, my brothers, sisters, mothers and fathers," he said eyeing a few of the older ones. "It gives me no greater joy than to lead you as I have done for many years. I consider you all my blood. Closer than family. That's why it saddens me deeply to find out that a traitor is among us." Malik eyed the two cops but continued to walk around the inner area of the circle, looking at each of his gang members. "I've said it, and I will say it again. Any one of you who thinks he is ready to take this staff from me, come and get it. But have the gall, the balls, the sheer grit to face me. Many years ago, I held a head before you. You've seen the video. Still to this day it is spoken of, for no other has come close to the act. I could have done the same with Torrence. Taken his place by force but what good would that have done? I wouldn't have earned your respect. Instead, like all of you I rose through the ranks by getting my hands dirty with blood." Malik stretched out a hand. "When the time was right, Torrence handed over the reins freely, and all of you accepted me. That's the way it has always been done. Anything less than that is cowardice and deserving of nothing more than death."

The crowd cheered in agreement.

With that said, Malik dropped the staff and stepped back. He turned to Runt and nodded. Two large knives were handed to him. Malik dropped one and stepped back.

"Jamal, step forward."

The crowd turned, a look of astonishment on their faces. Each one singled out a six-foot-tall man lying on the front of a '60s green Chevrolet Impala. He wore a black T-shirt, with tight black jeans and the latest Nike Airs. He slid off the front and walked out into the middle as Malik turned over the knife in his hand.

"We know the penalty for being a traitor is death by the rest of the gang. Under any other circumstances that's how this would play out. Except it's you, Jamal. My right-hand man. The one person I trusted. So I consider myself a fair man. You want the staff? Come and take it."

Malik kicked the blade on the ground towards him. It clattered and stopped a foot from his boots. Jamal looked down and glanced around at the faces of those he called friends. Many had their guns at the ready.

"You don't want to know why?" Jamal asked, crouching and scooping up the knife.

Malik shook his head. "It's all the same. Power. Greed. Ego. Take your pick."

Jamal chuckled and lunged forward scything the air

with the blade. Malik moved fast slamming the back of his fist into the side of Jamal's temple, then following through with a back kick. Jamal hit the ground and the crowd roared.

"Come on, get up," Malik said, his eyes darting between Jamal and his guests. He could see the look of horror on their faces. This was foreign to them. But to his people it was what set them apart. Violence was an everyday occurrence, though against your own it was rare. Jamal rose to his feet and came at him again, slashing the air, dodging a few of Malik's punches and managing to connect one of his own. Malik wiped blood from his mouth and smiled. "Nice shot."

This time he attacked, cutting Jamal three times. Once across the abdomen, and twice across the back. Bleeding and in pain, Jamal took a second to catch his breath before feigning an attack, only to throw his knife. Fortunately, Malik anticipated that being an option and moved swiftly to the right. The knife struck the hood of a car and bounced off, disappearing below a vehicle. Jamal stretched out his hands. "Go ahead."

Malik knew what he was doing. Baiting him into a kill that would only work against him in the eyes of his gang. He wouldn't do it. Instead, he tossed his knife near Jamal's feet. "Try again."

This time it was Malik who opened his arms.

Jamal looked at him, then sneered as he reached down and scooped up the knife. In one smooth motion, as he turned to get some distance, he spun around and fired it at him. Malik twisted, slapped it in midair then rushed at him tackling him to the ground. They wrestled and fists connected in one final fight for control. All the time Malik got the better of him. Jamal wasn't street hardened. He'd always fancied himself as a gangster, worn the colors, said what needed to be said to gain attention and for a while even pulled the wool over Malik's eyes, but he wasn't gang material. Not really.

At some point in the fight, Malik got on Jamal's back and put him in a choke hold. He clenched his arm around his throat and held him. All the while as he choked the life out of him, he spoke into his ear so only Jamal could hear. "I trusted you. I would have given you the reins but you chose this, and for that…you give me no other choice."

Jamal's body went limp and Malik continued to hold him until he knew he was dead. Once there was no movement, Malik rolled out from underneath him and rose to the cheers of his gang. He glanced over at Nick before lifting a hand and swirling it. "Let's ride out!"

Chapter 13

It was hard to imagine life could get any worse. Miles away from her family, lost in a city she'd never visited, pursued by military and surrounded by the deranged, Jenna didn't sleep well. None of them did. They'd arrived at a home just off Calumet Avenue. It was two doors down from a Baptist church. The two-story home looked out across an empty green, and towards Washington Park, a place they had almost died in the previous night. Unbeknownst to them it wasn't a place to linger even in the daytime hours due to muggings but now with the city broken by an outbreak, it was filled with lunatics, and the desperate looking to take advantage.

When they arrived at the home, Sergio had broken in and searched it before they entered. The place had been locked up and had a few cans of food, the leftovers of a family that had packed up their belongings and fled the city, at least that's what Lars thought. Awake in the early hours of the morning, Jenna looked at the family picture on the mantelpiece. She was standing in the living room of a spacious abode full of top-of-the-line furniture. No expense had been spared and it was clear the family enjoyed the finer things in life. Even though both she and Brody had held down good jobs, even they weren't in a position to purchase some of the items found inside — Persian rugs, antique and historic décor, solid wood floors and pricey high-end kitchen appliances.

"You miss your family?" Sergio asked. Startled, and unaware that anyone else was up, she nearly dropped the framed photo. Jenna turned to see Sergio leaning against the French doors that separated the living room from the corridor.

"Yeah."

"But I don't see a ring on your finger."

"My husband and I are going through a separation."

"Ah," he said strolling in and running his hands over the spines of books on the shelf while glancing at her in a way that made her feel uncomfortable. "You mind me asking what led to it? You know, the finer details."

"That's not really any of your business."

"Fair enough," he said smiling and sinking down into one of the overpriced chairs. "Man, I could do with a cigarette."

"There are some cigars in that drawer behind you."

"Really?"

He got up and took a look, pulling out a small humidor and cracking it open. Inside were a handful of Cuban cigars. Sergio took one out and ran it beneath his nose, savoring the smell. "Now that is quality. You smoke?"

"Nope but don't mind me." She put the frame down and walked over to the window and looked out.

"How was it last night?" she asked.

Sergio and Lars had rotated in shifts to make sure they hadn't been followed by the military and to watch over her while she slept. Unlike them she was drained. Constant tests had exhausted her. But that was all part of the testing procedure. Keeping her mind under stress, putting her into scenarios of fight-or-flight.

"No sign of them. Though there are a lot of infected out there." He got up and walked over, puffing away on his cigar and glancing at it every few seconds. He'd roll it around and then spit with little disregard to the home he was in. "My biggest concern is not the military. Anyone with a lick of sense isn't going to get caught out in this. Which reminds me. You know we can't go back to Alpine."

"We have to."

"You heard Lynch. They've wiped Alpine and Marfa off the map."

"I have to know what happened to my son and..." She was about to say husband but stopped. It had been a long time since she'd referred to Brody as her other half. A long time since she'd had feelings for him beyond anger. There was so much pent-up pain inside of her, she didn't know what to do with it except bottle it up and push it down.

"Hey, you got a cigarette?"

Lars wandered into the room.

"Over there. Cigars. Help yourself," Sergio said without looking.

Lars glanced at Jenna and smiled. She considered herself a fairly good judge of character. Lars was different from Sergio. Less threatening. Kind even. "There's two cans of peaches left in the cupboard if you want them for breakfast."

"Not really a peaches guy," Lars said, then wandered over, struck a match and puffed away. He rubbed his eyes. "Man, I need to get some sleep. Being awake half the night isn't good for me. I'm starting to think this was all a bad idea."

"Bad idea?" Sergio said. "C'mon Lars, you know as well as I do that eventually they would have run out of food, been overrun by the infected or had desperate people show up at their door. What then? You can be sure they would have taken that helicopter and left us. No, what we did was for the best."

Lars sat down on the window seat and peered out.

"But where now?"

"We were just discussing that. Jenna here wants to return. I'm telling her it's not in the cards. I say we find a safe zone."

"And how do you expect us to find that?"

"There is a convenience store not far from here. I say we check it out. See if we can't get our hands on a radio. There has to be someone broadcasting."

"A radio? No need to risk that. I found one in the bathroom," Jenna said. She walked off and went upstairs, only to return a few minutes later holding a bathroom radio. "Battery powered." She turned it on and began surfing through the channels. Nothing but static came out. No local station. Nothing.

"Well I guess that answers that," Lars said.

Jenna was just about to give up when the static disappeared and a broadcast was being played. "If you are hearing this. There is hope. We are a small community located in Maine. There currently are no infected here. We have been able to cut ourselves off from the mainland. We welcome new people, especially anyone who is a doctor, nurse, police officer, military or has a trade that can be of use. We don't let anyone in but if you have something to offer, we will chat with you. Come to Ellsworth, Maine, head south past Trenton and across the water to Thompson Island, it's just before Mount Desert Island. You won't be able to go any further than that so don't even try. Our people will be there to greet you. I repeat. If you are hearing this. There is hope."

The message replayed on a loop.

They looked at each other and Sergio smiled. "I told you. We're heading to Maine."

"Oh great. Well let me just load up the family car and we'll head out," Lars said before rolling his eyes. "Are you out of your mind? We have no transportation, and the nation has crumbled."

"You don't know that."

"Look around you, Sergio."

"That's Chicago. This place was bound to collapse in on itself. It was already teetering on the edge."

"Yeah, whatever," Lars said. He rose from his seat and headed into the kitchen to root around.

Sergio followed him in as did Jenna. There wasn't much there when they arrived. A moldy loaf, a bottle of olives in the fridge, milk gone bad and some expired chicken pieces in the freezer. The rest had been taken by the family.

"To be honest, I'm surprised this home wasn't broken into already."

"People would go to the stores first," Jenna said. "Then hotels, anywhere large amounts of food could be."

"So we raid a few homes, fill our bags and hike out of here. Maybe we get lucky and find a vehicle along the way that has gas in it."

"Yeah, and maybe the world goes back to normal by noon," Lars said shaking his head as he took out the peaches. "Oh, look what we have here." He reached into the back and dug around and then pulled out a half-eaten packet of Doritos.

Jenna frowned. "Seriously, you aren't going to…"

"Nothing wrong with them," he said fishing into the bag. He pulled out a handful and shoveled them into his mouth. There was no crunch. The air had got to them and made them soft. He chewed for a second or two then grimaced and spat them out. That's when they saw that some of the packet had rat droppings in it. "Ah fuck," Lars said. "Nasty."

Sergio cracked up laughing and patted him on the back. "I told you to watch where you stick your hand."

"That's what she said," Lars shot back before both of them chuckled. Jenna pursed her lips and walked away. They were like two teenagers. As she made her way back to the rear of the house, she came out into the hallway and was going to use to the second bathroom when she froze. She almost ran into the man. A stranger stood before her with a gun in hand, pointing at her. He had greasy hair that came down to his shoulders and he smelled worse than a landfill. His brown clothes were tattered and torn, and his skin dark and patchy. Had she seen him on the street she would have thought he lived there.

"Don't move," he said in a quiet voice. Behind her she could hear Lars and Sergio chatting and Jenna knew she was out of sight. He motioned her to come to him and she thought about bolting for a split second but she knew that if that gun was loaded, she'd be dead before she'd made it a few steps. With his hair strewn down over his face it was hard to see if he was infected or not. Everyone was living in fear, everyone could have been infected.

Jenna took a few steps until she was within arm's reach and the man wrapped his arm around her, clasped his hand over her mouth and walked back slowly until they exited the house. All the while Jenna's eyes bulged. Inwardly she was screaming for Sergio or Lars to walk around that corner but they didn't.

* * *

Sergio was the first to notice. He'd been in the habit of keeping a close eye on Jenna ever since they'd left the facility. If she was meant to be the hope that turned this shit around, he fully intended to make damn sure nothing happened to her. Of course his motives weren't exactly pure. He planned to capitalize on the great white hope. That's why he'd been up early that morning, and that's why he never let her out of his sight for more than a few minutes at a time. When he bedded down for the night, he'd had Lars watch over her and instructed him to wake him if he thought she was about to run.

Frowning Sergio stepped back into the room. "Lars. Where is she?"

"What?" Lars said, puffing away on his cigar.

Sergio glanced into the kitchen, then called out to her before bursting outside and looking around. He took two steps at a time until he was on the sidewalk and then glanced both ways. "Jenna!" he yelled before hurrying across the street.

Lars tossed his cigar to the ground and dashed after him. "Sergio. Get inside. We'll have a better view from above."

"She's got to be out here. She was only out of my sight for a couple of minutes."

Farther up the street a group of three individuals spotted them and began to run towards them. "Sergio!"

Sergio saw them coming and darted back around the house one over from them to avoid their pursuers knowing which house they came out of. As soon as they were around the back they scaled the fence of the neighboring house and got back inside, and locked the door behind them. "Shit. Shit!" Sergio cried out as he rushed up the stairs to the second floor. As soon as they got up there, they used a chair to reach a skylight that gave them access to the roof. Within minutes they were up and had closed it behind them. Sergio darted over to the edge of the roof and peered over. Below, the three lunatics came rushing down with a baseball bat, chain and large machete in hand. They watched as the lunatics followed their path. Though when the men reached the rear of the home, instead of climbing the fence they burst into the second home.

A few screams split the silence, and then there was quiet.

They watched and waited until the men emerged covered in blood and satisfied. They glanced around, looking for more victims before running south down Calumet Avenue.

Lars frowned. "Strange. It's like they're acting as one."

"Maybe. Maybe not. Perhaps they don't lose their sense of who they are. Just what they're fearful of, or angry about. You remember Jenna saying that the disease affects the amygdala and memory," Sergio said, rolling over and sucking in the chilly Chicago morning air.

"Speaking of Jenna —"

Before Lars could finish Sergio cut him off. "She's probably run off," he said. "I knew this would happen."

"She wouldn't do that," Lars said scanning the area from the east side.

"No? And you would know?"

"She might have been eager to escape the facility but she isn't stupid. There's a reason she went with us and not by herself."

"Well that's simple. I knew the way out."

"Please. Give her some credit."

Sergio ignored him and checked the other side of the building. He wanted to go down, search for her, but Lars was right, it wasn't safe out there. At least not in daylight. They were too easy to spot. At least at night they had the cover of darkness.

While they were checking both sides of the house and calling her name, Sergio heard what sounded like a helicopter approaching. "Lars, you hear that?"

"I don't hear anything." He walked over to the skylight and opened it to get down.

"Look," he said pointing to the east. Sure enough coming towards them was a Chinook helicopter.

Chapter 14

A walk in the park. More like pure hell. Twenty-one minutes. That's how long it should have taken to get to the University of Chicago Medical Center. Traversing the dangerous streets of Chicago wasn't easy when in the company of gang members but in a lawless city, free of police or anyone to step in and intervene, it was pure insanity. Brody rode in the same vehicle as Malik. He saw him glancing in the rearview mirror every few seconds. Uncomfortable with the situation and what Emerick had shared that morning, his mind had been at a loss for what to do. Emerick's plan B turned out to be pure horseshit. Nothing more than a concoction fueled by watching too many bad thriller movies. It wasn't practical and it sure as hell didn't take into account the glaring fact that they were still unarmed. None of their weapons had been returned to them and for good reason. Malik wanted to make damn sure they weren't giving him a line about a cure.

Brody looked out and saw three people looking in a store. The front window had been smashed in and nearby bodies lay strewn across the sidewalk — fresh kills? The convoy of a dozen vehicles navigated around abandoned ones, and didn't slow down for even a second.

"You look worried," Malik said.

"Me?" Brody replied.

He nodded with a grin.

"Just..." Brody trailed off, his mind was on numerous things, mostly the safety of his son, and the well-being of Jenna. Gottman could be right. There was a chance she could be dead. Who knew what kind of tests they had run on her or once they'd extracted the cure, whether or not they would leave her alive? "I just want to get this day over with."

"I hear you."

"That man back there that you killed. Who was he?" Brody asked.

"A close friend of mine. We'd known each other since

we were young. He was meant to be in line for leadership, I guess he never fully got over it when I took the spot."

Brody glanced at Gottman beside him and Gottman said, "I wanted it but not bad enough to kill you." Both of them chuckled. The laughter soon subsided.

Brody looked down at the floor of the vehicle and then back at Malik.

"Look, um. There is a chance they haven't found a cure."

"What?" Malik replied, turning in his seat. He was sitting in the passenger side as one of his men drove the black sedan. There were multiple cars ahead of them and even more behind.

"What I'm saying is there are those who are immune but that doesn't mean the military have managed to figure out why. Look, I know you don't owe us anything, and I appreciate all you've done but we've got kids among us and if you're planning on—"

Before he could get the words out, there was a sudden burst of gunfire. It felt like hail hitting the vehicle. It was coming from above and behind. The vehicle they were in swerved and crashed into a parked truck. Brody looked up and saw that their driver was slumped over the wheel, multiple rounds riddled his body. The windshield had numerous holes in it. He glanced up and behind and saw that the other vehicles were also coming under fire.

"Raymond. Drive, you idiot," Malik said reaching over only to have his body fall on top of him. "Shit!"

"He's gone," Gottman said.

All Brody could think about was Nick in the vehicle behind them.

An onslaught of gunfire assaulted them, peppering the vehicle. He knew that if they didn't get out they would soon be killed themselves. The problem was getting out meant being exposed and they didn't even have weapons to protect themselves.

"DeMar," Malik shouted. "We need cover."

DeMar was one of his men in the back with them. He nodded and pulled the Uzi submachine gun strapped to his shoulder around and opened the door. He didn't even manage to get his head out of the vehicle before he was killed. DeMar slumped half in, half out of the vehicle, his body still being hit by rounds.

"Pull him in!" Brody yelled to Gottman

"He's dead."

"I have an idea."

Malik looked back. Gone was the hard exterior. Here he was isolated in a vehicle in the middle of Chinatown being shot at by unknown assailants.

"Anyone know who the fuck is shooting at us?" Gottman shouted.

"It's the Latin Eagles," Malik replied. "They're the only ones in this neck of the woods."

"And you didn't think to pick a different direction?"

"It's the only way south after that blockade."

The back window exploded and shards of glass rained over them.

Brody reached over and grabbed the Uzi out of DeMar's hands. Malik looked at him and for a second, he knew Brody could have killed him but instead he turned and fired randomly out of the rear window to try and push back.

"Listen up. You see that building over there," Brody yelled. "When I say, you'll have to make a run for it."

"Are you out of your mind?" Malik shouted, ducking his head as another stream of rounds lanced the vehicle.

"You want to die with your men?"

Malik shook his head.

"Then when I say go. Run."

He ducked as another hail of gunfire pelted the car. Brody glanced out and saw where they were positioned on the tops of the roofs. They had driven into the fatal funnel. Behind them, the same situation was taking place. "Go!" Brody yelled as he returned fire. Malik pushed out as did Gottman and they darted towards a building that had the front window kicked out. On the outside, the sign said ZERO. He had no idea what it was, only that it was cover and right now they needed to get out before they all died.

As soon as Malik was out of sight, Brody followed suit.

He wanted to rush back towards the vehicle behind him but there were too many shooting from above. He could barely escape with his own life. He darted into the building and came to discover it was a karaoke bar and club.

* * *

Nick, Devan and Jasper were slammed back into their seats as the driver stuck the gearstick into reverse and tried to back out. It was a flawed plan. They smashed into the vehicle behind them and the engine died. Nick glanced out and saw his father run into a building across the street. Devan was cursing up a storm as he caught sight of assailants on the ground shooting into the vehicle behind them. He leaned forward and grabbed a hold of the guy driving the vehicle and begged him to give them a weapon.

It was pointless, the guy wouldn't listen. Instead he got out of the driver's side and within seconds was dead.

"Fuck this!" Devan yelled. "Jasper, reach through and grab his gun."

Jasper cowered. He shook his head.

"If we don't get a weapon we die."

The final gang member in the passenger side shot at the windshield and used his boots to kick it out before attempting to scramble out. It was useless. Another heavy onslaught of rounds finished him off leaving him bleeding to death. Nick reached forward and grabbed the Glock out of his hand.

"My father is in that building. Listen up. I'm going to use that guy's body to cover us. The chances of us making it out of this alive are slim but we have to try."

Both of them nodded as Nick slipped from the rear to the front and pulled the dead man in. He unlocked the side door and pulled the man's body over him as he fell out onto the sidewalk. With a gun in one hand, and the man within his grasp, he tried to get a bead on who was firing at them. The body shook several times as rounds hit the guy in the back. As scared as he was, Nick was determined to live. "There's no way in hell I'm dying out here," he said. "Jasper, Devan. Let's go." He hauled himself up using the man's dead weight as a shield as they backed out. They made it a few steps before Jasper was hit. He spun like a spinning top, collapsing to the ground only to be hit again with another round, this time in the back.

"Jasper!"

"Devan, run," Nick shouted. There was no time to mourn or even help their friend. The gunfire was steady and furious. Behind them many of Malik's men had got out and were returning fire, it all seemed to play out in slow motion. In the short time he was out in the open, he witnessed man after man lose their lives. They dropped like flies in the hail of bullets. The odds were stacked against them. The gang had driven into a fatal funnel and even though there were a dozen vehicles containing four people to a vehicle, it wasn't enough to prevent the massacre.

Nick glanced at Jasper as he dropped the dead guy and ran for the building. Jasper wasn't moving. Within seconds he was in the door and gasping for breath. His father grabbed him and hugged him hard.

"Where is Jasper?" he asked.

He shook his head and looked at Devan who was standing by Emerick. Emerick, Callie and Chad had managed to break away from the gang. Chad slammed the door behind them while Emerick stood by his son. The noise of war outside was overwhelming. Glass shattered, holes appeared in vehicles and gun shells clattered off the ground. Malik stared out shaking his head as he watched his men get torn apart.

"We can't stay in here. They'll be looking for us," Malik said, leading them out the back. Exposed, on foot and with only the weapons they'd managed to grab from the fallen, they emerged out of the back and ran at a crouch towards Canal Street. Malik knew the streets like the back of his hand. He guided them away from the sound of war towards a yard full of shipping containers. They were by the rail line that ran parallel to the I-90 express. Darting into there and finding cover behind hardened steel, they stopped running and took a moment to catch their breath.

* * *

"Why are you heading south?" Gottman asked.

"You want to get to the CDC, right?" Malik said.

"But your men…"

"My men knew what they signed up for."

Brody nudged Gottman and shook his head. All he was concerned about was making it alive to the CDC and if anyone could get them there it would be someone native to the city. As they trudged on Brody noticed that Callie was in tears. He motioned to Nick to comfort her. "Go speak with her."

"Me?"

"You like her, right?"

"Yeah but…"

"Go speak with her."

He listened in as Nick pulled back and walked beside her. "You okay?"

She shook her head but said nothing.

"You want to talk about it?"

Again, she shook her head. Nick strolled back up to where his father was.

"She won't speak."

"Too traumatized," her father said.

"Did she know Jasper well?"

"I don't think so."

Losing Jasper was hard but it was to be expected. Not all of them would make it out of this new world. They were lucky they had even made it this far. The pandemic was spreading, getting worse, and many had fallen prey to it. Bodies lay strewn all over the ground. Nick's father said it was the seventy-two-hour period, but that didn't explain why there were still hundreds of infected out there. They'd seen them on the way into Chinatown. They'd even seen some drop as bullets were exchanged.

For the next hour they walked the train line, staying away from the city streets in the hopes of reducing the amount of confrontations. Malik said nothing as he led the way. No matter how much of a wall he tried to put between them, Nick could tell he was affected by the death of his men. Guilt could eat a man alive and in a society that had collapsed there was more than enough of that to go around. Nick wondered what was going through each of their minds as they walked in silence surveying a city ablaze. Smoke spiraled overhead, and the sound of gunfire persisted.

"How long until we reach it?" Nick hollered.

Malik didn't look back. "Twenty minutes by car. Roughly two hours by foot."

Nick grimaced, the thought of being out in the open for two hours was terrifying. It wasn't just the infected they had to deal with now but the gangs. Nick shuffled forward and caught up with Malik. He fell in step, only looking back a couple of times to check that the others were okay.

"Why are you doing this?"

"Doing what?"

"Helping us."

"I said I would."

"Emerick overheard one of your men talking about

killing us regardless of whether or not you found the cure. Is that true?"

He scoffed. "What my men talk about isn't my business."

"It seemed like your business when you killed your pal."

Malik shot him a sneer and Nick's lip curled. "Careful."

"What? What are you going to do? All I want to know is would you have ordered it?"

Malik shot him a sideways glance. "Does it matter now?"

"Yeah. Yeah it does."

He looked as if he was about to answer when Chad caught sight of a group up ahead. "Guys. Move it." They hurried towards one of the many trains that had been abandoned on the tracks. They dropped down while Chad, his father and Emerick climbed up and positioned themselves at the ready.

As they waited there in silence, Nick turned to Malik.

"So?"

"Kid, you really don't give up, do you? Yes. Yeah, I would have ordered it."

"I knew it."

"If…" Malik trailed off. "You had attempted to screw us over. I don't kill without reason."

"Of course you do."

"Then you have misunderstood how gangs work."

"Oh, I know enough. Drive-bys, people wearing the wrong colors, allegiance to the wrong gang, walking through the wrong neighborhood."

"You think we took you in because you were a threat to us?" Malik asked.

"What other reason was there?"

Malik shook his head. "Let it go, Nick. You have no idea."

Nick wanted to say more but the group of strangers was getting closer. They were infected, close to ten of them, each holding different weapons in their hands. Rifles, shotguns, knives, chains, bats and wooden staffs.

"Before they used to attack each other. Why not now?" Callie said.

"I don't know. Maybe the disease has modified itself," Gottman said.

The group prowled with a wolf pack mentality. A few ran ahead scouting while others hung back. When they were parallel to the train, Nick pulled back so he couldn't be seen but prepared to open fire if need be. Fortunately, they were lucky, no one dropped anything and the group continued on, searching out its next kill, whoever that unlucky individual would be, he was just glad it wasn't them.

Chapter 15

Jenna heard Sergio calling out but she couldn't respond. The stranger had one dirty, smelly hand wrapped around her mouth while the other pressed the barrel of a gun into her neck. He'd moved fast. Taking her to Holy Trinity Baptist Church only a few doors down. She still had no idea who he was or what he wanted only that he looked out of his mind. The only upside was that if he was infected, she wouldn't contract the infection. The sound of a chopper circling overhead could be heard then it disappeared. Once the man was satisfied that no one would enter, he pushed her down on the ground and straddled her back. For a moment she began to think the worst. Every possible scenario played out in her mind. He was going to stab her, shoot her in the back or sexually assault her. None of that happened. He kept repeating to himself, "I'm so glad I found you. I've been searching for you for days. I thought I had lost you forever."

"Mister, I think you have me mixed up with someone else."

"No. I would never forget my Shelly."

He took some torn strands of material and tied her hands behind her back before twisting her over and seating her in one of the pews. He then proceeded to pace back and forth scratching his head. When he turned away, Jenna noticed that he was bleeding on the back of his head.

"You know, I can look after that for you. You wouldn't want that to get infected," she said motioning with a nod. He slowly stopped scratching and then darted to one of the windows and looked out. He looked like a paranoid mental patient. But the more she looked at him the more she began to realize that perhaps he wasn't infected but just someone who'd lost his mind in the whole ordeal. Grief had a way of doing that. She thought back to losing Will. At first she couldn't comprehend he was gone. She lived in denial. She refused to see his body, and wouldn't let anyone near his room. Over the months that followed, she spiraled down, even beginning to talk to him as though he was alive. Maybe that's why Brody distanced himself from her. He tried to reach out to her to get help and utilize a psychologist but she refused. It took her four months before she finally snapped out of the state she was in and accepted help.

"What's your name?" Jenna asked as she tried to untie the binds behind her back.

"I..." He tapped the side of his head as if it wasn't working. "Harrison."

"Harrison...?"

"I..." It was clear his mind had been affected in a deep way. He teared up and wiped his face with the back of his dirty sleeve.

"Tell me about Shelly?"

"You already know."

"No I don't."

"Stop it. Stop it!" he shouted crouching down and putting both hands over his ears.

"Okay. Okay. I just wanted to hear from you. Am I your daughter? Wife?"

She began to act as if she'd somehow forgotten. He looked at her with a frown and then got up and came over. "My daughter. You're my daughter."

Jenna nodded. "That's right. I'm your daughter. Shouldn't you untie me if I'm your daughter? These really hurt."

He shook his head and backed away, this time heading for the door.

"Harrison. I mean, Dad," she said correcting herself. He stopped with his hand on the door and looked back. "Please. Don't leave me here."

"You'll be safe. God will look after you. I need to find your mother."

Jenna leaned forward "But she's here."

He frowned. "Nancy is here?"

"Yeah," Jenna said.

He stepped away from the door and looked around. "No. No, you're lying, she's not." Jenna could feel the knot beginning to loosen. A few more seconds and she would have it untied. She just needed to buy herself a little time.

“Dad, she’s out back.” Jenna made a nod towards the rear. She felt sorry for him but anyone who would tie up their own daughter couldn’t be trusted. Anyone who would show up out of the blue and hold a gun to her head couldn’t be trusted.

“Out back?”

Jenna nodded. Harrison looked at her skeptically before slowly making his way towards the area of the church building that was used for the pastor and staff. He disappeared into the corridor and the door swung shut. Right then, Jenna moved fast, she dropped to the ground and managed to get her wrists under her feet. At which point she could see the material. She pulled at the material with her teeth until it came loose. A quick tug and the bind fell away. As soon as she was free, Jenna dashed towards the exit. She burst out and turned straight into him. A hard whack to the head and her legs buckled.

The last thing she remembered was him leering over her. "I trusted you. I trusted you. Now father must punish you."

Total blackness closed in at the corners of her eyes and then she lost consciousness.

* * *

Sergio and Lars stayed low on the roof as the Chinook helicopter flew overhead. While face down, Lars had heard a scream but was unable to pinpoint where it came from and they didn't want to get up and risk being seen. They waited until the helicopter disappeared into the distance before rising and making their way down.

"That was them, wasn't it?" Lars said.

"Of course. They're out looking for her."

"We need to get out of here."

"Forget it. We need to find Jenna," Sergio replied.

Lars shook his head. "She could be miles from here by now."

They headed down to the lower floor. They hadn't made it but a few steps when a figure shot out, charging into Sergio. Knocked back against the wall, Lars jumped in to help but was pulled back by two more. The same men they'd seen earlier had entered the house. In all the noise of the helicopter they hadn't seen or heard them enter.

Sergio kneed one in the groin and as he buckled, drove his knee up into his face. He quickly pulled his Glock and fired a round into the guy's face, then pushed forward into the room. Two men were holding Lars, his arms stretched apart. One of them held a machete to his gut.

"Put it down!" Sergio yelled. They just stared blankly as if lost in some weird dream. "Did you hear me?" he shouted moving forward. The one guy jabbed the knife against Lars and he let out a cry.

"Just shoot them," Lars yelled, trying to pull away from the men. As he aimed his gun at the one, a fourth man charged at him from another room farther down the corridor. Sergio reacted, unloading a round and dropping the guy before he could get within four feet of him.

Turning back, he saw that Lars had managed to free an

arm and had cracked the one guy holding the machete in the face. But Lars wasn't fast enough for the second assailant who fired point blank into his gut, not once but twice. Sergio rushed forward, rage gripping him, and unleashed every bullet he had in the Glock into the man who'd shot Lars.

He dropped down to his knees and immediately put a hand on Lars' side.

"No. No, you're gonna be okay."

Lars looked at him, barely able to form a word. He sucked in air fast.

"Stay with me. This is just going to be like last time. You remember that guy in Alpine who shot you. We managed to…" Sergio saw that he was losing him. He couldn't lose him. He was the only friend he had. He tore off his shirt and pressed it against the wound that was bleeding out of control. Lars' eyes rolled back in his head and he slumped to one side. Sergio slapped him a few times on the face. "Wake up. Wake up. Stay with me!"

His eyes opened and a wave of fleeting hope filled

Sergio's being.

"Sergio," Lars muttered. Sergio stooped low and got his ear close to Lars' mouth. "Find Jenna. Get her to safety. For all the wrong you've done. Do something right."

Sergio nodded. "We'll get her to safety."

"I'm afraid not this time, my friend. This is as far as I go."

"Don't talk like that. Just stay still. I'll get help. I'll go find her. She's a nurse, she'll know what to do."

Lars gripped him and shook his head. "Promise me."

"Promise? Shut the hell up. You're not dying."

"Promise me," Lars said.

Sergio gripped his bloodied hand and nodded.

Lars gave a strained smiled one final time and then his hand weakened and he slipped away.

Chapter 16

Brody squeezed off a round into the face of the lunatic. His adrenaline was pumping, his senses on high alert on the final leg of the journey. Although the two-hour trip to the CDC located in the University of Chicago Medical Center had been far easier than driving. Being on foot made it easier to see threats coming, and the various routes they could switch to were numerous compared to the narrow roads. Still, it hadn't been a walk in the park. The streets south of the shipping canal were filled with the infected — people so deranged and out of control they attacked without hesitation.

Sweating, out of breath and gasping for air they'd made it to an area just north of the university called Drexel Square when they found themselves being chased by a group of over fifty people.

At some point, they'd become separated.

The last time Brody saw him — Nick, Callie and

Devan were fleeing from a group of ten, heading towards a block of apartments. Chad and Emerick were driven west on Hyde Park Boulevard and Brody, Gottman and Malik were running south down Drexel Avenue.

"I've got to go back for my kid," Brody said.

Malik shouted at him. "There's no time. Quick. This way!"

Either side of them were apartments as far as the eye could see. Most were used by students attending the university. With thirty people on their ass they didn't have the luxury of trying to catch their breath or run in another direction. They weren't going to make it to the university so Malik decide to enter a gated courtyard to their left. A black sign above the gate read Heritage on Drexel. Malik slammed the gate closed but it wouldn't lock.

Four of thirty people reached them before the others did. They charged into the fence, a look of fury masking their faces. One of them stabbed at Brody through the gate with a samurai sword. Gottman unloaded a round taking him out followed by another to the guy who was trying to push his way in.

"This way!" Malik yelled rushing over to a door. "Damn it! It's locked."

"Stand back," Gottman said as he took a few shots at the door. It did nothing except create holes. He kicked it several times while Malik and Brody held off the slew of attackers who had now reached the gate and were pushing against it. The bars of the fence began to give. It was only a matter of time and the sheer force of them pushing would bring it down.

Brody looked up and shouted. "Open up!"

"I'm trying. This damn door won't budge."

Suddenly they heard a buzzer sound and the door clicked open. Within seconds all three of them entered and closed it behind them. They didn't stick around to see if the angry group would breach the gate. As soon as they came around a corner, further down they saw a young guy wearing a mask and waving them on. "Down this way." All three hurried just as they heard the sound of beating against the access doors.

Within minutes they entered an apartment on the ground floor.

* * *

Devan swung the hammer across the guy's face taking out his jaw. Nick followed through with a round to the heart. They made it inside the apartments but were now being chased up the stairwell. Nick tried to keep his eyes on the way ahead but Devan was having trouble holding back the surge of eight who were lashing out with steel pipes, and what looked like table legs. One of them struck Devan in the gut, and had Nick not been armed, he could have easily been beaten to death. Instead Callie pulled Devan to safety while Nick unloaded every round he had left in the Glock in each of the seven remaining lunatics. They fell back, some dying immediately, others writhing and bleeding out. The sound of more entering the apartment block made it even more terrifying. Backing into a corridor, they didn't bother trying to find something to block the door with, there was no time. All three of them dashed to the far end hoping to escape through the exit but it was already ajar, and as they got closer, six more enraged men and women entered. Nearly stumbling over each other, they turned and hurried back the other way but by then more had flooded in, trapping them. Nick aimed the gun and squeezed the trigger. It clicked but nothing happened. He was out of ammo.

"Shit."

"Come on, you fuckers!" Devan said slapping the hammer against his palm. Pinned in the middle of a corridor full of apartment doors, Nick began banging. He turned a few handles while keeping an eye on the deranged.

Keeping Callie between them, Devan faced one way while Nick faced the other. Out of ammo he had nothing except his fists.

"You want some of this!" Devan said swiping the air.

Callie banged on a door. "Open up. Please. Open."

"There's no point. Even if someone is inside they aren't going to risk it. They don't know if we're infected or not," Nick said.

Still, she paid no attention and turned to the next door and did the same. Nick and Devan prepared for the worst as the group of people ran at them. No one would come to their rescue, no one would open the door and save them at the last minute. Nick slammed into the first one using his longest tool, his leg. He kicked the guy in the nuts and followed through with an uppercut. He didn't turn to see how Devan was doing but he could hear him screaming and cursing at the top of his voice.

All the while Callie continued beating on the doors, hoping, praying that someone would show mercy and open. When it happened, it wasn't anyone they might have expected to come to their aid, it was an old lady. And she wasn't bearing a gun, or anything that would protect her. She came out with a hard-bristled broom in her hand.

"Get inside," she yelled.

They didn't hesitate even as the woman was overwhelmed by the lunatics.

"Lady!" Callie shouted.

But she was gone, swarmed by the infected. Nick slammed the door shut only to feel the masses beating on it from the other side. "Get something. Anything to block this door." Every kick against the door was jarring. It wouldn't hold long but maybe long enough for them to escape.

* * *

Multiple attempts to get inside buildings failed. Emerick and Chad kept moving. Neither of them had a weapon. Ten infected had given chase, one of them had a rifle and kept firing rounds. How they managed to avoid being hit was a mystery or an act of God. They zigzagged, darted up alleys and tried to pull on door handles. Eventually Chad scooped up a garbage can and lobbed it through a window of a local garage, and they climbed inside hoping to elude their pursuers.

Emerick immediately picked up a tire iron, and tossed a hammer to Chad.

They backed up and took cover behind an old beat-up

red Ford truck that was in the garage for repairs. Behind the vehicle they heard the deranged run past the window. Emerick looked at Chad and shook his head. "If we ever get out of this, I'm going to do something different with my life. I swear."

Chad frowned. "Yeah, like what?"

"I dunno? Skydive. Climb a mountain." He smiled. "Join the military." The smile broadened and both of them laughed. Emerick peered around the truck. He couldn't hear anyone but that didn't mean they weren't out there. His thoughts were with his son, and the others. Had they managed to escape or were they overwhelmed? He couldn't entertain the thought of their demise. It was too much to bear.

"So?"

"I think it's clear."

They got up and went over to the window and peered out. Sure enough the group of lunatics was gone. "You know, Chad. Times like these make a person think about their decisions. I um…I think I may have misjudged you." Chad glanced at him and Emerick looked away.

"Emerick Jones. That wouldn't be an apology, would it?"

"Well let's not go that far," he said before chuckling.

Chad slapped him on the back. "It's all good, man. C'mon, let's get to the CDC."

* * *

When Jenna awoke, her head was throbbing. She reached up and noticed her hair was sticking to her face. When she pulled her hand away there was blood. She rolled over and threw up, retching several times. A quick glance around the room and she noticed she was in an office. There was a large desk to her right with a leather chair, a floor to ceiling shelving unit stacked with a library of books and a small window that let in sunshine. Her wrists and ankles weren't tied and Harrison wasn't there. The first thing she did was hurry over to the door and pull on it.

It was locked.

She gave it a few more tugs before backing up and

searching for anything she could use as a weapon. Surveying the room, there wasn't much except a lamp on the desk. She scooped it up and removed the top, pulled the plug and tied it around the base before scything the air a few times to see if it would do the trick. She'd make it work.

Right then she noticed a framed photo on the desk.

Jenna turned it around and that's when all the pieces fell into place.

Harrison was in the photo. He was standing in front of the church with his wife and daughter beside him. She glanced at the nameplate on his desk and then realized who he was — a minister. Another look at the photo and she could see why he thought she looked like his daughter. They were around the same build and height, had almost identical hair color and length and were similar in appearance. Of course, she wasn't her doppelganger but she could tell how under duress he might mistake her for his daughter.

Right then, she heard a key go into the lock and twist.

Jenna slid up beside behind the door, preparing to attack.

The door opened but no one stepped in. Jenna waited, gripping the lamp.

She heard movement, footsteps walking away from the door and then another door closing. Jenna took a peek into the corridor. There was no one there. What was he doing? Trying to lure her out so he could overpower her?

Adjusting her grip on the lamp, Jenna ventured out keeping her back to the wall as she moved down the darkened corridor. She'd take a few steps and then stop, listen and continue on. Up ahead was a set of double doors that would take her into the sanctuary, and at the far end just before the doors was another room that was used for kids.

The closer she got the more her heart sped up.

Her palms were sweating as she got nearer to the room.

One quick look inside and it was clear he wasn't in there which left only one more place. Jenna placed a hand on the handle and pulled. No sooner had she cracked it a few inches than he burst through knocking her to the ground. The lamp slid out of her hand and clattered to the floor, and he pounced on her. "Shelly, what did I tell you?"

"I'm not Shelly," Jenna screamed as he grabbed her by the wrist and began to drag her back to the office. For a man of his size he was strong.

"Stop lying. God doesn't like liars. What did I teach you about lying? What did I say would happen if you lied?"

Jenna tried to get up but he was dragging her so hard it was impossible.

After pulling her back into the room, he threw her down and proceeded to remove his belt.

"Spare the rod, spoil the child," he said as he folded the belt and snapped it a few times in his hands. Jenna scrambled to her feet and tackled him, driving him back into the wall. He gasped and threw her across the room straight over the table. The framed photo and a laptop computer clattered to the floor, and papers went everywhere. "Your mother was right. You don't learn. But I'm going to teach you."

What kind of insane upbringing did his daughter have? If she was now dead, perhaps she was finally free. Pain shot through Jenna's back as she tried to get up. Harrison was too fast. He reached around and grabbed her by the back of the neck and forced her over the table. Jenna drove her heel into his shin, and he let out a loud cry, buckling just a little. She scampered around the table and was heading for the exit when she felt something hard and heavy slam into her back causing her to hit the ground.

Before she could determine what it was, Harrison was on her in a flash. He lashed out with the belt straight across her back, and she screamed in pain. Another came seconds after. However, before he got a third in, a gun went off and she heard him collapse. Jenna turned and looked into his dead eyes before looking up and seeing Sergio standing in the doorway with a handgun outstretched.

He tucked it into the back of his jeans and crouched down putting a hand around her and raising her up. "It's okay. I got you."

Chapter 17

Inside the masked man's apartment Brody took in the sight of multiple rifles set up by the window. The carpet was littered with brass as if he'd been on a shooting spree for the better part of a week.

"The name's TJ Robinson."

He was close to six foot in stature, blonde hair, dark piercing eyes, heavily tattooed and barrel chested.

"I appr—" Brody was cut off.

"Four questions. Are you infected? Have you been exposed to the infected? Where are you from? Where are you heading?"

"Um," Brody looked at Gottman and Malik before he responded. "No, as far as we know we aren't infected. We have come across the infected but haven't been close enough to get infected. We are from Texas and are heading to the CDC."

"Why?"

Outside they heard the noise of the infected run past.

"It's a long story."

The man raised his gun. "I've got all the time in the world."

Gottman put a hand out. "Hey look, we don't mean you any trouble."

"Well you've brought it this way."

"We had no other option," Brody said. TJ's eyes darted to Malik who looked as if he was about to try and take him down. Instead, Brody intervened by stepping forward and putting his arm out. "Look. We just want to get out of here. That's all. You waved us in. We wouldn't be here if you hadn't."

TJ stared back intently before he shuffled backwards and glanced out the window. "Chances of you being able to make it to the CDC are slim to none. The streets out there are crawling. It might not look dangerous but they are watching." His eyes roamed the many windows of the building across from them. He released the drapes and looked at them again. "Why are you going there?"

"The cure," Malik said matter-of-factly.

"There's no cure for this," TJ shot back.

"There's a cure for everything," Gottman said, eying the weapons on the ground. "It's just a matter of whether or not they release it, and whether or not the damage can be reversed."

"On what basis do you make this claim?"

"My wife is immune," Brody said.

"Immune?"

"She doesn't show any symptoms of the disease."

"You know what this is?" TJ asked.

Brody shrugged. "A little. Enough. Enough to know if I don't find her there isn't any hope for us."

"Well why didn't you say so?" With that said, TJ scooped up a rifle and tossed it to Gottman. "You're gonna need that." He did the same with Malik and went over to his closet and pulled out a shotgun. "I gather you've used one of these before?" he said, handing it to him with a box of shells. "Fill your pockets and when you're ready we'll leave."

Gottman looked at Brody and it felt like they'd struck gold. Out of all the people they could have run into, this seemed almost too good to be true. "You ex-military?" Brody asked.

"No, just someone who likes to be prepared." He glanced at Malik and studied him. "You're with one of the gangs, aren't you?"

"You know me?" Malik asked.

"I recognize the tattoo."

"And what did you do for a living before this?" Brody asked.

TJ smiled and shook his head. "I'll get you to the CDC but let's understand one thing. I'm not here to hold your hand, answer twenty questions or take responsibility for your inability to take action. Clear?"

"Crystal," Brody replied.

TJ went back to the closet and pulled out a bulletproof vest and slipped into it. On the back of it were the letters DEA.

"You're with the Drug Enforcement Administration?"

"No but my brother was. This is his condo."

"Where is he?" Gottman asked.

TJ shot him a glance. "What did I say about questions?"

"Right." Gottman frowned and looked at Brody. They weren't sure what to make of him. Still, they weren't going to rock the boat. They needed weapons and someone willing to watch their backs.

TJ walked over to the window and looked out. "We're leaving on foot but you need to follow me."

"Hey, I already know these streets," Malik said.

"Then you won't have any problem following me," TJ muttered before unlocking the double doors that led out to a courtyard in the rear of the condo. "Whatever happens. We don't stop for anything or anyone. I mean it."

"You're the boss," Gottman said grinning. "Lead the way."

TJ stared at him for a second and then flung the door wide and they rushed out, immediately firing at the infected that had gathered.

* * *

The pounding on the door didn't let up. Although the locks were in place the sheer force of those pushing against the door meant it wouldn't hold forever. Callie and Devan shoved a sofa across the tiled floor. "Get out of the way," Devan said as they jammed it against the door and then they each grabbed anything they could find and stacked it on top. TVs, entertainment unit, chairs and home décor. They kept filling it up until they were confident it would hold. While they continued to do that, Nick went over to the French doors that led outside. Before he reached them, a man burst through wielding a hammer. He swung it and Nick tackled him to the ground only to look up and see another. Devan was on the next, using a knife grabbed from the kitchen. He stuck it into the woman's chest and kept pressing forward until she was back outside.

"Devan!" He turned and Callie threw him another knife. He moved out of the way and it clattered on the tiled floor.

"Holy shit. You want to kill me?"

"I thought…"

"Hand it over next time."

It was taking every ounce of strength in Nick to hold the lunatic below him at bay. He kept his arms outstretched and held him down keeping his face away. The last thing he wanted was to get infected and this guy was all spit and blood.

"Devan," Nick shouted. In the next moment the infected man let out a cry after Devan stuck him in the side with another knife. There was no time to linger. They hurried out, running away from the building.

Chapter 18

Brody was the first to arrive at the CDC. They killed six infected people on the way in before finding the stairwell. They stepped over the bodies of military, and many doctors whose heads had been crushed. Blood was everywhere. It looked as if a massacre had occurred.

"Holy crap," Gottman said as they ascended the steps and began to clear each of the floors. As they went, they soaked in the chaos. The walls were peppered with rounds, and in every direction, bodies lay in various states. It was a sickening sight.

Malik didn't say anything but by the look on his face, Brody could tell he wasn't optimistic. "Jenna!" Brody yelled as he went floor to floor. No one was alive. Patients, doctors, nurses, military and security guards had been butchered. Blood was smeared over the walls and floors.

"Brody," Gottman said holding a clipboard in his

hand. He turned it and at the top of the sheet of paper was her name. Below, a chart was filled out with medical terminology, check marks and x's. He wandered through the corridors checking each of the rooms, searching for survivors, anyone who might tell them where Jenna was.

TJ cradled an AR-15 in his arms and hung back surveying the area for threats.

With every floor they cleared, Brody's hope of finding Jenna dwindled. Even if she had been there, was she now among the dead? Would they have to check every body to make sure that she wasn't one of them? The thought of finding her dead crushed his spirit. His nerves were already on edge at the thought of losing his son but going on without both of them was hard to even comprehend.

By the time they made it to the last floor he had resigned himself to the fate of not finding her. "I'm sorry, Brody," Gottman said. "We tried."

He nodded and they began to make their way down.

"That's it? No cure?" Malik asked.

"Give him a break," Gottman said.

"A break? I've just lost over forty of my men for what? Nothing?"

Brody stopped walking and looked at him. "I didn't guarantee you anything. You knew that when coming here."

"All I knew was you were touting a cure."

"Yeah, well it's not here," Brody said walking on. "And that cure, is my wife."

He pushed through into the stairwell to be greeted by the sight of Emerick and Chad raising their guns. "Whoa!"

"Holy shit, you scared the crap out of us," Emerick said. "Who the hell is this guy?" he asked looking at TJ.

"Long story. Is my son with you?"

"No. I thought he was with you."

"They broke off back at Drexel."

"Shit!" Emerick said hurrying down the steps.

"Wait up," Brody yelled, dashing after him.

"I can't lose him."

They didn't have to travel far. By the time they made

it to the bottom floor, there were their sons, out of breath, sweating and terrified.

"Dad," both Nick and Devan said at the same time.

Brody and Emerick hurried forward and embraced their sons.

"You okay?" Brody asked.

Nick nodded. "For now. We managed to outrun them but there are others coming."

Gottman chimed in. "We need to leave the city immediately."

Brody frowned. "But Jenna…"

Gottman took a hold of Brody and pulled him to one side. "We tried to find her. We gave it our best shot. Now if we want Nick to stay alive, we need to start thinking about ourselves."

Brody knew he was right but it was hard letting go. They'd come so far. Outside they heard the sound of gunfire, and TJ and Malik hurried over to the front entrance and looked out. "We need to leave now!"

"Dad. Where's mom?" Nick asked.

He grimaced and shook his head.

"She's dead?"

"I don't know."

"Where are you heading?" TJ asked.

"East. Towards Maine. There is a safe zone," Nick said.

"And you know this because?"

"It's being broadcast on the radio."

TJ chuckled. "And we're just meant to believe that? Like we're meant to believe there is a cure? Look how this worked out. You expect me to traipse across miles of chaotic country on a whim?"

"No one is asking you to do shit," Brody said, stepping to his son's defense. "That's where we are heading. If you wish to come. Feel free."

TJ eyed him and sighed. He looked at Malik. "You going?"

"Haven't decided yet."

"Well you better choose soon as we are leaving now," Gottman said hurrying towards a set of doors. He opened one and waved them on. "You coming or not?" Brody, Nick, Devan, Emerick, Chad and Callie all hurried through the door. Gottman stood there waiting. "Suit yourself."

They ran down the corridor only to hear the other two following.

Brody left that day broken. They all did. Jasper was gone as was his wife. His mind was in turmoil. Questions circled as to the whereabouts and fate of Jenna. In some ways it might have been easier to accept had they found her dead. It was the unknown that tore at his heart. He wanted to believe he could save her— that he could bring his family back together and restore what the years had stolen but he had to be realistic. The hope of them living out a normal life was gone, the nation was no longer stable. The cries of the infected echoed in the medical center as they fled.

Tomorrow didn't offer much, nor did the safe zone in Maine guarantee them survival and safety but as long as he was breathing, he would do everything in his power to protect what remained of his family.

* * *

Several miles away, Jenna and Sergio trudged through the streets of Chicago searching for a vehicle with fuel in the tank. Neither one had spoken much since the Baptist church, neither one had seemed in any frame of mind for conversation. Sergio opened the door on a beat-up VW Beetle and smiled. He jangled the keys before turning it over to see how much gas was in the tank. The dial rose to just under half a tank. "About time! Jump in."

Jenna hopped in the other side and Sergio swerved out into the street and headed east doing his best to avoid any crowds or blockades. Jenna brushed dust and grime off her legs.

"What you did back there. I appreciate it," Jenna said casting him a glance.

He nodded but didn't say anything.

"Lars. What happened to him?"

Sergio sighed. He was hesitant at first to speak but then began to bring her up to speed. As he unloaded his burden, she saw another side to him that he hadn't shown in the time that Lars was alive. Buried below the hardened walls he'd erected to keep her at a distance was someone who felt pain, someone who cared. And had he not shown up when he did, there was a good chance she wouldn't be alive. She owed him her life, that was for sure.

"Are we going to return to Alpine?" she asked.

Sergio shook his head. "No. It's gone."

"But it might have been a lie. The towns could still be there."

"No, I heard it on the radio. Most of the West is gone. Buried beneath death. However, there was a signal that was being broadcast. There is a safe zone in Maine, on Mount Desert Island. I don't know about you but that's where I'm heading. If you want me to drop you off somewhere, I would understand."

Jenna didn't respond to that immediately. She needed to sit with it, think about the gravity of the situation, the reality that had befallen the country. She'd heard the colonel talking on the radio to someone on the Chinook as they arrived in Chicago. She'd heard the conversation clearly mention the destruction of the two towns. She wasn't sure whether to believe it or not. Had Brody managed to get out in time? Not if he thought she was in Alpine. Had her son survived? The chances were slim to none. As a mother she didn't want to let go. She didn't want to grieve over something she wasn't certain about, but the reality was this was a new world that didn't function the way it did before. And even if they had survived, did they even know she was here? Too much time had passed and the country had collapsed in on itself. Traveling back to Marfa with nothing more than a hope or a prayer was too risky.

What if they were attacked along the way? What if they reached Marfa and it was all gone? She didn't think she could take that much grief. All she could do was take it a day at a time and hope they were still alive. She had to believe they'd been taken in by one of the FEMA camps and would eventually be reunited.

It was a pipe dream at best but one she would cling to.

"So, what's it going to be?" Sergio asked pulling over to the side of the road. Jenna looked out and back at Sergio. Here was a man carrying similar grief to her. At least she felt safe with him.

"Maine. Let's go to Maine."

Chapter 19

24 hours later

Mount Weather

"You lost her?" the president bellowed at her in person. Colonel Lynch dropped her chin as she received the full berating. She'd expected Mosley to find Jenna but the city was too vast and there were too many threats on the ground — far more than they had imagined. They'd already lost three good men to the lunatics on the lower ground floor of the medical center, and many more after that as the stairwell was breached and the facility overrun.

Had it not been for the Chinook on the roof she had no doubt in her mind she would have joined them. Lynch could still hear the screams of doctors and nurses as the infected forced their way in and attacked each level. She'd been waiting for an update from Mosley when it happened. Only once had she given the command to the pilot to touch down and that was to pick up Mosley on the way out. Even then they had to fight back a crowd that tried to get close to the helicopter. "I'm sorry, sir. We did everything in our power," Lynch said. He scoffed, shaking his head as he walked the full length of the boardroom. His Joint Chiefs of Staff were there, as were Mosley and Margaret Wells from FEMA. Lynch knew returning empty-handed wouldn't go down well even though they had twisted the events that led up to the breach. It was partly their own fault. Though Mosley wouldn't take responsibility for it.

"Then we will have to move ahead with plan B," he said turning to Margaret. She nodded and walked over to a computer and pressed a few buttons. On the screen before them a video began streaming.

"Plan B?" Lynch asked as she turned her head to look at the video footage.

"While you were wasting time trying to find a cure, we were putting into place additional safe zones on islands just off the coast of the U.S. The only way to see the survival of this nation is to isolate survivors. It will give us a way to ensure no more breaches happen and yourself and your team can continue to work on discovering a cure with the immunes."

"But we don't have any more immunes."

"You don't. We do."

"I'm sorry, sir, I don't understand. We're not going to continue to operate out of Mount Weather?"

"I will, but you will be going here," he said pointing to the footage. A drone hovered over an island showing numerous towns, and a lush forest surrounded by ocean. "Everything has already been set up. You will receive your briefing in the next hour and will be leaving at zero five hundred hours." He turned and motioned to Margaret. "Margaret will explain the rest to you. We have work to do."

Lynch rose from her seat. "Sir. You haven't said where I'm being sent?"

He stopped at the door and turned. "Mount Desert Island. Maine."

* * *

THANK YOU FOR READING

Please take a second to leave a review, it's really appreciated.

Thanks kindly, Jack.

A Plea

Thank you for reading Unhinged: The Amygdala Syndrome book 2. If you enjoyed the book, I would really appreciate it if you would consider leaving a review. Without reviews, an author's books are virtually invisible on the retail sites. It also lets me know what you liked. You can leave a review by visiting the book's page. I would greatly appreciate it. It only takes a couple of seconds.

Thank you — **Jack Hunt**

Newsletter

Thank you for buying Unhinged: The Amygdala Syndrome book 2, published by Direct Response Publishing.

Click here to receive special offers, bonus content, and news about new Jack Hunt's books. Sign up for the newsletter. http://www.jackhuntbooks.com/signup/

About the Author

Jack Hunt is the author of horror, sci-fi and post-apocalyptic novels. He currently has three books out in the War Buds Series, Four books out in the EMP Survival series, Two books in the Against all Odds duology, Two books in the Wild Ones series, three in the Camp Zero series, five books out in the Renegades series, three books in the Agora Virus series, and multiple single novels. There is one called Blackout, one called Final Impact, one called Darkest Hour, one called The Year Without Summer, one out in the Armada series, a time travel book called Killing Time and another called Mavericks: Hunters Moon. Jack lives on the East coast of North America.